NICK AND TESLA'S

ROBOT ARMY RAMPAGE

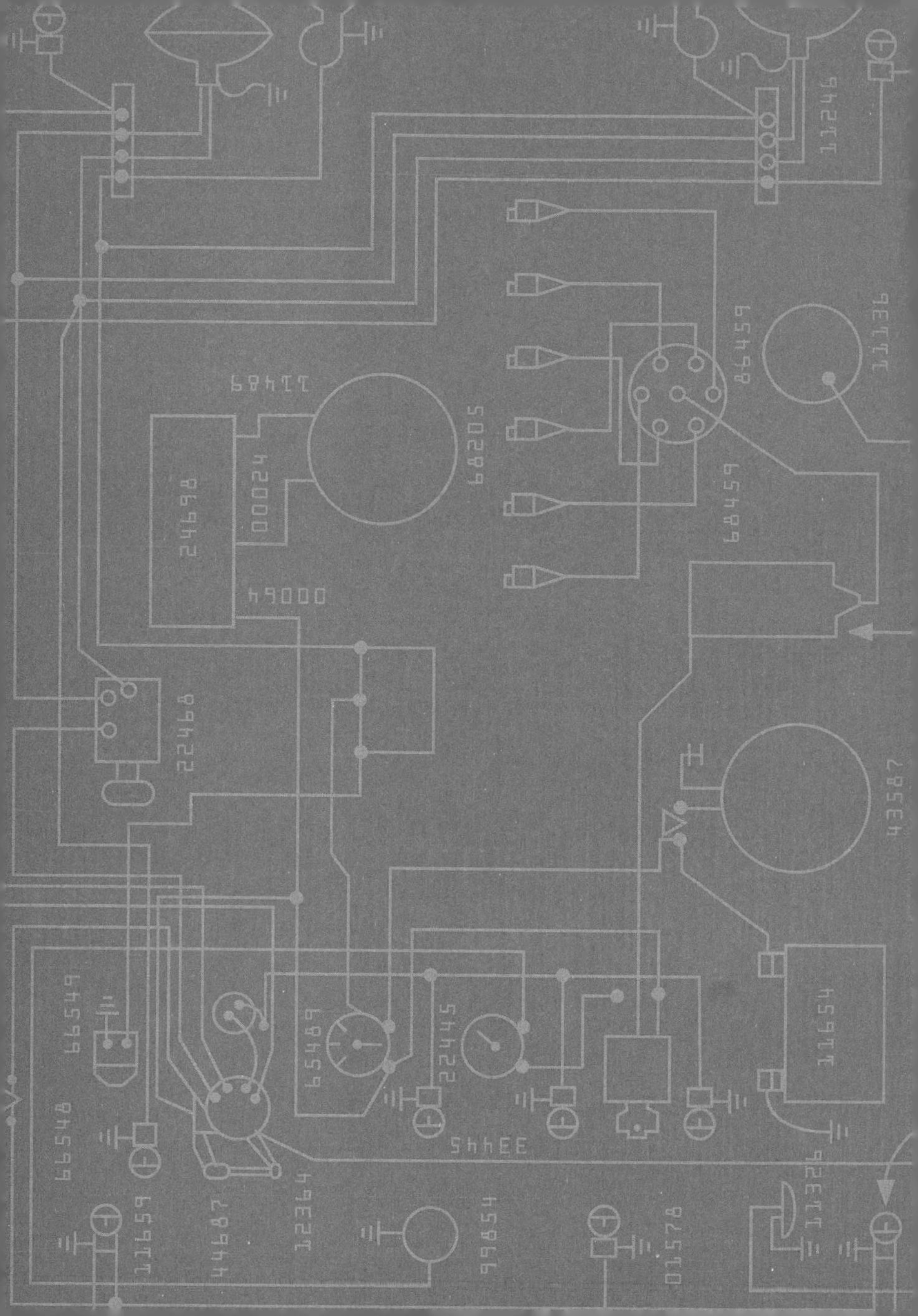

NICK AND TESLA'S

ROBOT ARMY RAMPAGE

A MYSTERY WITH

HOVERBOTS, BRISTLEBOTS, AND OTHER ROBOTS YOU CAN BUILD YOURSELF

BY "SCIENCE BOB" PFLUGFELDER AND STEVE HOCKENSMITH

ILLUSTRATIONS BY SCOTT GARRETT

Library of Congress Cataloging in Publication Number: 2013943365

ISBN: 978-1-59474-649-9

Printed in China

Typeset in Caecilia, Futura, and Russel Square

Designed by Doogie Horner
Illustrations by Scott Garrett
Production management by John J. McGurk

Quirk Books
215 Church Street
Philadelphia, PA 19106
quirkbooks.com

10 9 8 7 6 5 4 3 2 1

DANGER! DANGER! DANGER! DANGER!

The how-to projects in this book involve electricity, toxic substances, sharp tools, contents under pressure, and other potentially dangerous elements. Before you build any of the projects, ASK AN ADULT TO REVIEW THE INSTRUCTIONS. You'll probably need their help with one or two of the steps, anyway.

While we believe these projects to be safe and family-friendly, accidents can happen in any situation, and we cannot guarantee your safety. THE AUTHORS AND PUBLISHER DISCLAIM ANY LIABILITY FROM ANY HARM OR INJURY THAT MAY RESULT FROM THE USE, PROPER OR IMPROPER, OF THE INFORMATION CONTAINED IN THIS BOOK. Remember, the instructions in this book are not meant to be a substitute for your good judgment and common sense.

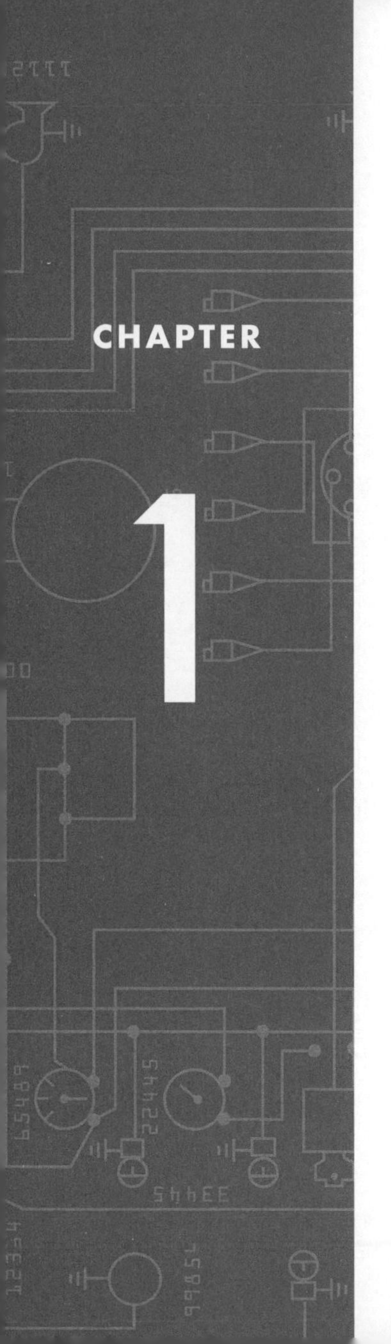

Nick was in the lab in the basement making a volcano with vinegar and dish-washing liquid.

Tesla was in the lab in the basement making a rocket with vinegar and baking soda.

Uncle Newt was in the lab in the basement making a compost-fueled vacuum cleaner out of a leaf blower and a bag of putrid bananas.

It was the vacuum cleaner that exploded.

Fortunately, the Banana Vac 8000 began sizzling and melting before exploding, giving Uncle

Newt time to groan, "Aww, man. Not again."

Nick and Tesla knew what that meant. They put down their beakers, test tubes, and tongs and hurried toward the rickety stairs. They had to do a lot of zigzagging, as the dimly lit basement was packed with old computers and grimy tools and abandoned inventions (a rocket-powered skateboard here, a gumball machine stocked with goldfish there) and, along the walls, mysterious contraptions that hummed and throbbed and occasionally went *ping*. Some of the machines were scorched. All were covered with soot.

"Come on, Uncle Newt!" Nick said as he and his sister began bounding up the steps.

Uncle Newt was the kind of man who needed to be reminded that it's a good idea to leave when a vacuum cleaner is about to explode.

"I just don't understand," he said as he reluctantly rose from his cluttered worktable and followed his niece and nephew. "I had the oxygen/methane mix perfect this time."

"That's what you said *last* time," Tesla pointed out.

"I know! It was perfect then, too."

Nick and Tesla scrambled up to the landing at the

top of the stairs and turned to find their uncle plodding along behind them.

"Uhh, Uncle Newt?" said Nick. "Maybe you want to move a little faster?"

Uncle Newt swiped a hand at him dismissively. "Oh, I've still got at least five more seconds to get away. Maybe even six. Well, four now."

The kids retreated into the kitchen, and slowly, serenely, he followed them.

"Two," he said. "One."

Nick, Tesla, and Uncle Newt stood for a moment, staring at each other. Then there was a *whomp* that shook the whole house.

"See?" Uncle Newt said. "There was plenty of time."

Smoke rose from the basement. It smelled like a hundred burned banana cream pies sitting in the sun at the county dump.

"Eewww," said Uncle Newt, grimacing and pinching his nose. "That's even worse than usual. Come on."

He led the kids out to the backyard, leaving the door open so the smoke could swirl out instead of filling the house. Uncle Newt's hairless cat, Eureka, trotted after them, curled up on the porch, and began

licking ash off his wrinkled, bald butt.

It was a bright, warm summer day, and one of Uncle Newt's neighbors—a genial old man Uncle Newt always called Mr. Blackwell, even though his name was Jones—was mowing his lawn nearby.

Mr. Jones stopped his mower and pointed his inch-thick glasses at Uncle Newt and Nick and Tesla.

"Need me to call the fire department again?" he said.

"No thanks, Mr. Blackwell," Uncle Newt told him. "It's just a methane-rich banana mash reacting to oxygen and putting out a lot of carbon dioxide and water vapor."

"Oh," Mr. Jones said, nodding and smiling and clearly not understanding a word. "All right, then."

"Don't worry about the smoke," Uncle Newt went on. "That'll probably stop in an hour or so."

"An hour or so?" someone said.

Uncle Newt and the kids turned around to find another neighbor, Julie Casserly, glaring at them. She was crouched by the side of her house, planting a new bed of begonias to replace the one that Uncle Newt's (supposedly) self-steering lawn mower had chewed through two weeks earlier.

Julie coughed melodramatically, then jabbed a trowel in the direction of the foul-smelling smoke billowing out of Uncle Newt's back door.

"You expect me to put up with *that* for an hour?"

"Of course not, Julie," Uncle Newt said. "You could always go inside."

Julie shot to her feet and did just that. But there was something about the way she snorted and scowled before she stomped off that made it clear she wasn't retreating from just the smoke.

"Who do you think she's gonna call?" Tesla said.

“The fire department or the police?”

“Both,” said Nick. “And probably the Pentagon and the White House, too.”

Mr. Jones started his mower again.

“I could modify that so it’d mow the lawn *for* you, Mr. Blackwell!” Uncle Newt bellowed at him.

Mr. Jones just waved and went back to cutting grass. He obviously knew better than to let Uncle Newt anywhere near his lawn-care equipment.

“Oh well,” Uncle Newt said. “Time for Italian, I guess.”

“What?” Nick and Tesla exclaimed.

Uncle Newt sucked a lungful of smoky air in through his nostrils.

“I don’t know about you,” he said, “but I’ve got a sudden craving for Ranalli’s chicken vesuvio.”

Nick and Tesla blinked at him. Neither had any idea what chicken vesuvio was, but they did know this: Ranalli’s Italian Kitchen had great pizza.

“Let’s go,” Tesla said.

It was 10 o’clock on a Sunday morning—not the time most people chose to go out for Italian food. But if there was one thing Nick and Tesla had learned since coming to live with their uncle two weeks before, it was that he wasn't most people.

"Great!" Uncle Newt said. He pulled the lapel of his lab coat over his mouth like a mask. "You two pour a gallon of grease into the car. I'll go get the electro bib. I've been meaning to try it out in a restaurant."

He walked toward the smoke still roiling out the back door.

Tesla grabbed his right arm. Nick grabbed the left.

"Maybe you shouldn't go back in there till you can see what you're doing," said Tesla.

"And, you know . . . breathe?" said Nick.

Uncle Newt mulled it over while Nick and Tesla watched him anxiously. Not only were they worried about him asphyxiating in the house, they didn't want him bringing his electro bib—which was supposed to teach kids to eat neatly by giving off a shock every time a crumb touched it—to the restaurant.

Uncle Newt was a messy eater, and it was no fun listening to him yelp all through dinner.

"All right. We'll go without the electro bib," he finally said. He looked down at Eureka the cat. "*Stay.*"

Eureka finished licking his butt and trotted off toward Julie's begonias, looking like he was going to either eat them or fertilize them.

"To the Newtmobile!" Uncle Newt said.

The Newtmobile was a dent-dimpled green and brown monstrosity Uncle Newt claimed to have built by combining a broken-down Volvo, an army surplus Jeep, and a boat. As it putt-putt-putted up the street, Nick watched out for dogs behind them. Uncle Newt had converted the car's diesel engine to run on cooking oil instead of gasoline, and because he often collected his fuel from fast-food joints—most of which were happy to have someone haul off the grease they'd otherwise need to dispose of themselves—the fumes that spewed from the muffler smelled more like extra-crunchy french fries than carbon monoxide. Which was why it wasn't uncommon to look back and find a drooling collie or spaniel or Chihuahua charging after the car, a leash dragging behind it and no owner in sight.

There were no dogs today, though a determined squirrel kept pace with them for almost a block. Fortunately, it fell behind and presumably went back to gathering nuts by the time the Newtmobile reached

the Pacific Coast Highway, the busy state road that cut between Uncle Newt's neighborhood and downtown Half Moon Bay, California. Nick had been worried that he'd have to get out and chase the squirrel away before it could lock lips on the muffler and be dragged off to its doom.

These were the sorts of problems a person had when living with Newton Galileo Holt, a.k.a. Uncle Newt. Back home in Virginia, Nick hadn't had any problems at all. (Or so it seemed to him now.) But then his parents, both scientists working for the U.S.

government, had suddenly announced that they were being sent to Uzbekistan to study soybean irrigation, and Nick and Tesla were shipped off to California to spend the summer with an eccentric inventor uncle they barely knew.

Nick had never liked soybeans. Now he hated them.

There was a silver lining to living with a mad scientist, though. Nick and his sister had mad scientist leanings themselves, and they quickly made themselves at home in their uncle's basement laboratory. But that didn't make up for the friends they wouldn't see for months, the home they missed, and the mom and dad in a land so distant and isolated it didn't even seem to have telephone lines.

Nick and Tesla hadn't heard their parents' voices since the day they said goodbye two weeks earlier.

A pink blur flashed before Nick's eyes, and he heard his sister say, "Call 911. He's in a coma."

Nick blinked, and the blur came into focus.

Tesla was waving a hand in front of his face.

They were parked in front of Ranalli's Italian Kitchen, yet Nick was still staring blankly out the back of the Newtmobile.

"Hellll-loooooo?" Tesla said. "Anybody home?"

"No," said Nick. "I'm not home. But I wish I were."

Tesla took away her hand and gave her twin brother an understanding look. She was better at putting a brave face on things—better at being brave in general, actually—but Nick knew she was worried about their parents, too.

"Hey, look on the bright side," she said. "We're about to have pizza for breakfast."

Nick turned and started to scoot out of the car.

"You know," he said, "that's not a bad bright side."

But it was, actually.

Ranalli's wasn't open yet. If they wanted pizza and chicken vesuvio, they'd have to come back in an hour.

"Oh, well," Tesla said. "It was too early for pizza anyway."

"It's never too early for pizza," grumbled Nick.

Uncle Newt rarely offered them anything to eat that hadn't come out of a can or a box, and Nick was getting sick of Beefaroni and Froot Loops.

As he stared forlornly at the CLOSED sign on the restaurant's glass door, something inside the restaurant began moving.

"Hey," said Nick, squinting. "What's that?"

Tesla and Uncle Newt crowded in to peer inside, too.

“Is that a—?” said Nick.

“Why, yes it is,” Uncle Newt cut in.

“Whoa,” said Nick and Tesla together.

Marching around the counter by the cash register was a small, silver shape.

A robot.

It turned its glowing red eyes toward Nick and Tesla and Uncle Newt and stared back at them.

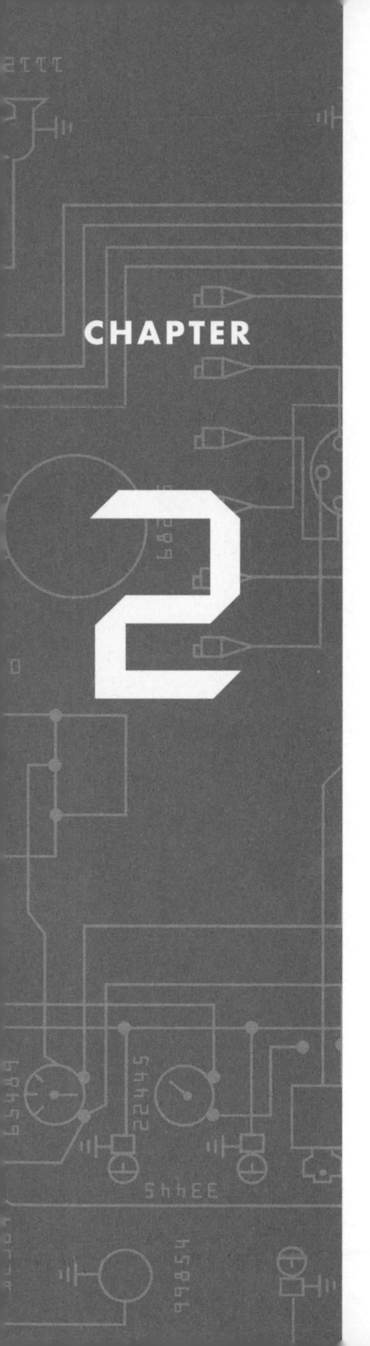

CHAPTER 2

The robot was about a foot tall, with a boxy body and arms and legs that looked like little silver girders. On top of its cylindrical head was a tiny chef's hat, and it wore an apron with RANALLI'S ITALIAN KITCHEN printed across it. One of its arms was raised, and spinning atop its metallic hand was a thin white disk.

The robot was twirling pizza dough.

"It just turned itself on," Nick said. "Like it noticed we were here."

"Motion sensor, maybe," said Uncle Newt.

"Cool," said Tesla.

She and her brother both liked robots. Yet despite all the gadgets they'd created together—and they *loved* creating gadgets—they'd never built their own robot.

Maybe it was time to do something about that.

"Uncle Newt," Tesla said, "can we go to the Wonder Hut?"

"Oh! Yeah! Can we?" Nick chimed in. "We're already downtown and we've got time to kill. Please!"

Uncle Newt turned away from the robot slowly, eyes wide.

"You know," he said dreamily, "I was about to suggest going there myself."

Nick and Tesla high-fived each other.

While most of the businesses on Main Street catered to the tourists zipping through town on the Pacific Coast Highway, the Wonder Hut was purely for locals. Eccentric ones, with a lot of time on their hands. Its musty, jumbled shelves were packed with model kits, toy soldiers, rockets, chemistry sets, electric trains, circuits, wires, and a long wall of radio-controlled cars, helicopters, planes, boats, and submarines. The place was cramped and dark and smelled like mildew and an old man's armpits, but that didn't matter. For kids like Nick and Tesla (and grown-ups like Uncle Newt), it was heaven.

"Are you thinking what I'm thinking?" Tesla said as they walked to the Wonder Hut.

"Are you thinking Uncle Newt's acting like a zombie?" said Nick.

"No! I'm thinking we need to build a robot of our own." Tesla glanced over at their uncle. "But you're right—he *is* acting kind of like a zombie."

A glassy-eyed Uncle Newt was shuffling along the sidewalk mumbling to himself. Only he wasn't saying, "Brains. Brrrraaaaaains." He was saying, "A robot that twirls pizza dough. Why didn't *I* think of that?"

"I doubt that was real dough, Uncle Newt," Tesla said. "And the robot was teeny."

"But it could be dough. And it could be un-teeny," Uncle Newt said, his haunted stare pointed at the horizon. "It could be *real*. A dough-tossing robot. Yes. Put some fake fur on it, and it could be a giant, dough-tossing mouse. Yes, yes, *yes*. Newtie, you're a genius! It practically sells itself!"

"It does?" Nick said.

Uncle Newt just went on talking to himself about how to build his giant, dough-twirling robotic mouse.

He was a tall, thin man with graying hair so messy it always looked like he'd just stuck his head out the window of a speeding car, and he was still dressed in the stain-splattered lab coat and slippers he'd worn that morning. So he was hard to miss as he shambled past the art galleries and bookstores and coffee shops lining Main Street. Tesla noticed tourists stopping to watch him expectantly, perhaps assuming he was a street performer about to launch into some kind of kooky act. It was a good thing she didn't embarrass easily.

"Uncle Newt," said Nick, who *did* embarrass easily. "Those things you're thinking about your robot? Did you know you're *saying* them, too? Out loud? So that everyone can hear?"

"Am I?" Uncle Newt looked surprised for a moment, then shrugged. "Well, you can't brainstorm without a little thunder. Now, where was I?"

"You were wondering how many servos you'd need on the arms to keep the dough spinning," Tesla said.

"Right! I could see getting away with . . . two, maybe. No, three! Definitely three! One here, one here, one here."

Uncle Newt began sketching an invisible diagram in the air in front of him.

"Thanks a lot," Nick grunted at Tesla.

She didn't answer. She was looking at something across the street, her brow furrowed.

Nick followed her gaze.

She was staring ahead at the Wonder Hut.

Nick looked at it, puzzled by his sister's reaction. Then his brow furrowed, too.

"Does the Wonder Hut look . . . different?" he said.

"Yeah," said Tesla. "It looks *clean*."

Usually the Wonder Hut had a grunge you could feel even before you stepped through the door. But now the building's grimy gray siding was blindingly white, and the letters on the sign over the door were crisp and black instead of illegible sun-faded smudges. And for the first time, the display window had a real display—an electric train running through a miniature San Francisco—instead of being jam-packed with stacks of old model boxes coated in a decade's worth of dust.

Nick and Tesla stopped to give each other a "what the heck?" look.

Uncle Newt just kept walking toward the Wonder

Hut—and the street.

"Don't forget to look both ways!" Nick called to him.

"But should the actuators be hydraulic or pneumatic?" Uncle Newt was muttering as he stepped off the curb. "Ooooh—or solenoids? I love solenoids!"

Nick and Tesla winced as cars in both lanes screeched to a halt to let Uncle Newt cross. He didn't even seem to notice when one of the drivers rolled down his window and called him what the kids could only assume was an extremely unflattering name.

The cars roared off with angry honks as Uncle Newt disappeared into the Wonder Hut.

"How old do you think Uncle Newt is?" Nick said.

Tesla knew what he was thinking.

"I don't know," she said. "But it's a miracle he's made it this far."

They looked both ways before crossing the street.

The Wonder Hut was as spic and span inside as it was outside. The walls had been repainted, the flick ery old fluorescent lights fixed, the shelves tidied, and the oldest unsold inventory—stuff that looked like it had been waiting for a buyer since before Nick and Tesla were born—replaced with brand-new models and rockets and kites and games. There was still a little whiff of mildew in the air, but at least the armpittiness was gone.

Even the guy behind the counter looked better, though it was the same employee they'd seen on previous visits. He was a short, jowly, bald-headed, stoop-shouldered man in his thirties or forties or fifties. (Nick and Tesla were bad at guessing ages.) Whereas before he'd kept his nose buried in a copy of *Miniature Railroading Monthly* or *Popular Mechanics* while they'd explored the store—and even when they'd tried to ask him questions—now he looked them in the eye and smiled.

"Welcome to the Wonder Hut," he said. "What can I do for you?"

"Oh, we're just looking," Nick said quickly. It always made him nervous when people in stores asked "What can I do for you?" It felt like such pressure. Couldn't people do their jobs without expecting an eleven-year-old to give them orders?

“Just let me know if you need any help with anything,” the man said.

He kept smiling at them.

Nick wished the guy would go back to reading magazines.

“I have a question for you,” Uncle Newt said from somewhere.

Nick and Tesla stepped around a rack of books with titles like *Detailing Your Realistic Sherman Tank* and saw their uncle standing near the back of the store.

“Where did this come from?” he said.

He was looking down at a squat, white, six-wheeled something-or-other that seemed to be looking back up at *him* from the store floor. Two stalklike arms protruded from the thing, and at the end of one was what looked like a camera—which was pointing up at Uncle Newt’s face. The other, slightly longer arm was straightening a display of role-playing games.

With a click and a *whirrrrr*, the thing rolled closer to Uncle Newt.

“Shake hands with Curiosity,” said the guy behind the counter.

“Pleased to meet you,” Uncle Newt said to the robot, and without hesitating he wrapped his hand around the gleaming pincers at the end of its longer arm and gave them a gentle shake. "I thought you were on Mars. And about five times bigger."

"Whoa! It really does look like Curiosity!" exclaimed Tesla, who considered the famous Mars rover one of her personal heroes, even if it happened to be a remote-controlled machine.

Nick's eyes went as round as a pair of silver dollars.

"I want to live here," he announced.

"In Half Moon Bay?" Tesla said.

"No. I want to live *here*. In the Wonder Hut. Do you think they'd let me? I'd figure out a way to pay."

There was a doorway at the far end of the store, just beyond Uncle Newt and the robot, and a woman stepped through the curtains hanging there. She was Uncle Newt's age—older than eighteen but younger than eighty—with short black hair and a round, pleasant face. She was carrying a little black box, and when she fiddled with a joystick mounted on it Curiosity rolled past her into the back room.

"Awwww," Nick and Tesla groaned, sorry to see the robot go.

"Awwww," moaned Uncle Newt, clearly feeling the same way. "We were just getting to know each

other."

"She'll be back eventually," the woman said. "I'm not done tinkering with her yet."

"When she is done, I'm history," the little guy behind the counter said.

The woman smiled at him. "You have nothing to worry about, Duncan. I'm not about to make Curiosity the Wonder Hut's assistant manager. She might be able to stock the shelves one day, but she can never know everything you do about model trains and airplanes."

"And remote-controlled cars," Duncan added. "And rockets."

The woman nodded. "Right. And remote-controlled cars and rockets."

"And model kits. And building ships in bottles."

The woman kept nodding. "And model kits and building ships in bottles."

"And—" Duncan began.

"Excuse me," Uncle Newt said to the woman, looking bewildered. "Are you the owner of the Wonder Hut?"

Nick was confused, too. He'd always assumed Duncan owned the place.

“The *new* owner, actually,” the woman said. “Mr. Kaufman, the original owner, wanted to retire, so he sold it to me. I used to be in here all the time when I was a kid, so coming back to Half Moon Bay to run the place is a dream come true.”

Uncle Newt stretched his hand toward the woman. Even from the other side of the store, Nick could see that it was trembling.

Shaking hands with a robot was no big deal to Uncle Newt. A woman, on the other hand, scared him.

“Well,” he said, voice quivering, “it’s nice to meet you, Miss—?”

“Sakurai. Hiroko Sakurai.”

Uncle Newt froze halfway through the hand-shake.

“Hiroko Sakurai? I know that name. It couldn’t be . . .” Uncle Newt blinked in disbelief at the curtains Curiosity had disappeared through, then turned toward the woman again. “But it must be! You came to the Jet Propulsion Laboratory—”

“Just a couple months after you left. Yes, Dr. Holt,” the woman said. She looked Uncle Newt up and down. “You *are* Newton Holt, I assume. You’re a bit of a legend down at JPL, actually. Mobility and Robotics Systems hasn't been the same since you left, apparently. I was hoping our paths would cross sooner rather than later."

"Well, consider us crossed, Dr. Sakurai! Our paths, I mean. This is such a treat! I haven't talked to anyone from JPL in ages. Tell me—how did you end up shielding Curiosity's computers from high-energy cosmic rays?"

"Well, the secret was switching to a slower, radiation-hardened microchip."

"Ahhh, of course. Go on!"

And the woman did. In detail. So much detail, in fact, that Nick and Tesla didn't understand 99.9 percent of what she was saying. As much as they loved robots, they couldn't follow a conversation about the advantages of high-gain over low-gain antennas for relaying commands via a deep-space network or why iridium made the perfect containment material for decaying plutonium-238 dioxide.

Duncan, the assistant manager, soon looked lost, too, and while his boss was distracted he slipped out a copy of *Model Yachtsman Magazine* and started flipping through it.

“Come on,” Tesla said. “Let’s go look at their micromotors and servo controls.”

“Good idea,” said Nick.

Yet when they got to the section where the components they needed to make their own robot should have been, the shelves and racks were bare.

“Oh, come on,” Tesla groaned. “Everything else in the store is new and improved, but they’re completely out of the stuff *we* want?”

Nick shrugged. “I guess we’re not the only ones in town who got the sudden urge to build robots.”

“Obviously not. But did they have to take everything?”

“They must have thought so. Whoever ‘they’ is.”

Tesla just growled. The mysterious “they” had really ticked her off.

She turned and marched back to the front of the store, Nick following behind her.

They found Uncle Newt and Hiroko Sakurai still so deep in conversation, they didn’t even notice Tesla the first two times she cleared her throat. The third time she tried to get their attention, her “*ahem*” was so loud Nick flinched.

“Oh. Tesla,” Uncle Newt said, finally looking her

way. "That's quite a cough you've got there. We'll have to get you some lozenges."

Tesla ignored him.

"We couldn't find any micromotors, servo controls, or actuators," she said to Dr. Sakurai. "Are you really all out?"

"I'm afraid we are. But there's more coming tomorrow, I think."

Dr. Sakurai turned to Duncan.

He managed to stuff his magazine back under the counter just in time.

"That's right," he said. "We'll be totally restocked by noon."

"Well, we'll just have to come back tomorrow then, won't we, kids?" Uncle Newt said with a smile.

"I'll be here," Dr. Sakurai told him. "Perhaps we could compare notes on kinematic functions for redundancy resolution."

"Perfect! It's a date!" Uncle Newt's face turned the color of strawberry jam. "A deal, I mean. It's a deal. Ta-ta!"

Uncle Newt hustled Nick and Tesla toward the door, then stopped and sighed once they were outside.

"'Ta-ta'? Really? 'Ta-ta'?" he muttered, looking profoundly disappointed in himself. "Well, let's go home."

"Home?" said Nick. "What about Ranalli's?"

"Ranalli's?"

Uncle Newt stared at Nick as if he'd said "What about the purple ostrich clown toast?"

"You know . . . Ranalli's Italian Kitchen?" Tesla said. "With the chicken vesuvio?"

"Oh. Right. Sorry. I guess I lost my appetite."

"But we haven't had breakfast!" Nick protested.

"Good thing we've got all that yummy cereal at home then, huh?"

Uncle Newt started walking back to the Newt-mobile.

Slowly, begrudgingly, Nick and Tesla followed.

Tesla talked her uncle into stopping for doughnuts on the way home. Yet Uncle Newt remained distracted and subdued even as he chewed on his cream-filled Bavarian, and Nick's chocolate-covered old-fashioned didn't seem to cheer him up, either.

When they got back to the house, they found that the smoke had cleared and the place smelled only *a little* like a rotten banana muffin burning in a campfire. Nick performed his usual ritual upon walking in the door—picking up the phone to check for messages—and, again as usual, he looked at Tesla and shook his head sadly.

Their parents still hadn't called.

Uncle Newt started to wander off past the stuffed polar bear and diving suit and stacks of beat-up computers and printers lining the hallway, obviously headed for the place he spent most of his waking day (and some of his nights, when he fell asleep at his worktable): the basement laboratory.

"What kind of idiot says 'ta-ta'? I *never* say 'ta-ta,'" he mumbled as he shuffled past a glum-looking Nick.

"Oh, snap out of it, you two," Tesla said. "It's time to build a robot!"

"But we couldn't get any parts from the store," Nick said.

"Since when have we needed parts from the store?" Tesla scoffed. "We'll improvise."

Uncle Newt had showed no sign he was paying any attention whatsoever. Just before he left the hall, though, he pointed at a stack of old PCs nearby.

"You could always use these," he said dreamily.

He waved a hand at an upside-down sombrero overflowing with electronics parts and pieces. "Or one of my spares."

Then he turned and headed down the steps to the basement.

"How could we build a robot out of that bunch of junk?" Nick said.

"Don't you want to find out?" said Tesla.

"I don't know. Maybe."

Nick began mooning at the telephone again, as if his sad puppy-dog eyes would convince it to ring. It didn't.

"Fine." Tesla stomped over to the sombrero and started sifting through the miscellaneous oscillators and capacitors and resistors within. "I'll build my own robot. I can make one better without you anyway."

"What's that supposed to mean?"

"Exactly what it sounds like. I've always been more interested in robotics than you. What could you suggest that I couldn't think of first and put together better?"

Tesla held up a small circuit board, examined it, then tossed it back in the pile when she noticed that one side seemed to be coated with dried ketchup.

"You're just trying to provoke me," Nick said. "You know I'm just as good with electronics as you."

"Oh? How much you wanna bet?"

Tesla gave her brother a hard, challenging stare.

He was right about her trying to provoke him. But that didn't matter.

Because it still worked.

"How about five million dollars?" Nick said.

Tesla shook her brother's hand.

"It's on, dude," she said.

NICK'S

DO-IT-YOURSELF PC LEFTOVERS WANDER-BOT

THE STUFF

- 1 3-inch (7.5-cm) fan from a junky old computer (or your local electronics store; the RadioShack part number is 273-243) (A)
- 4 wire coat hangers
- 1 9-volt battery
- 1 9-volt battery connector (B)
- 2 nuts (any size)
- 1 quarter
- Hot-glue gun
- Wire cutters
- Scissors
- Electrical tape
- Some extra wire

THE SETUP

1. Use the wire cutters to cut the straight part off each hanger, giving you four 10-inch (25.5-cm) lengths of wire.

2. Add a big dab of hot glue to one end of each wire. Let glue dry briefly. This will give "grip" to your robot's feet and will keep it from scratching surfaces.

3. Put the other, glueless end of each wire into the corner holes of the computer fan and glue them into place. Be sure the label side of the fan is facing down. Glue everywhere the wires touch the plastic so they won't come out or spin. When the glue dries, your robot will have legs!

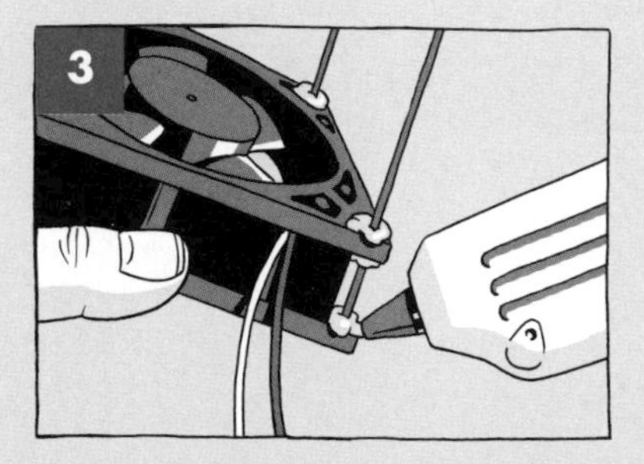

THE FINAL STEPS

1. Bend each wire leg so that your robot's "feet" are splayed slightly outward from the fan. This will increase your robot's stability. Also adjust the legs to ensure that all four feet touch the ground when you put down the robot.

2. Connect the 9-volt battery to the battery connector and tape the battery to the flat base at the bottom of the fan

(the part that does not spin). Make sure that the wires don't get in the way of the fan's movement.

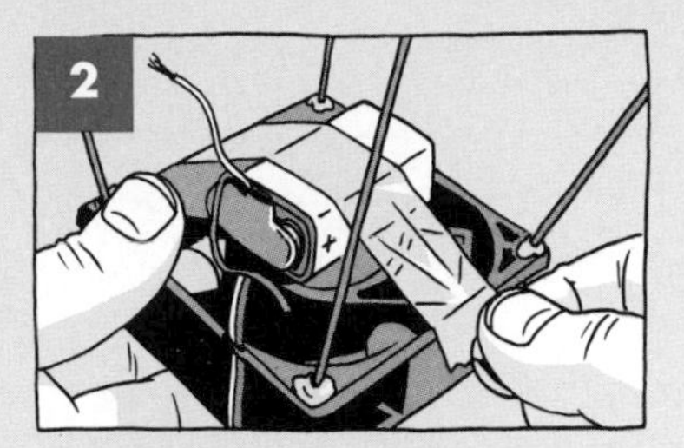

3. Wrap a few layers of electrical tape around the robot while pulling tightly to secure the legs and battery tape.

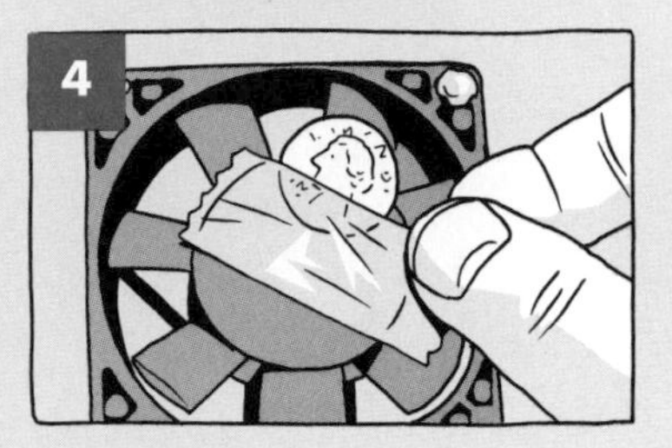

4. Glue the quarter onto the top of the fan so that it's slightly off center. Secure it with a piece of tape.

5. Glue the two nuts to the top of the fan (these are decorative "eyes").

6. Attach the positive wire from the fan to the red (positive) wire from the battery.

7. Connect the two negative wires—and stand back!

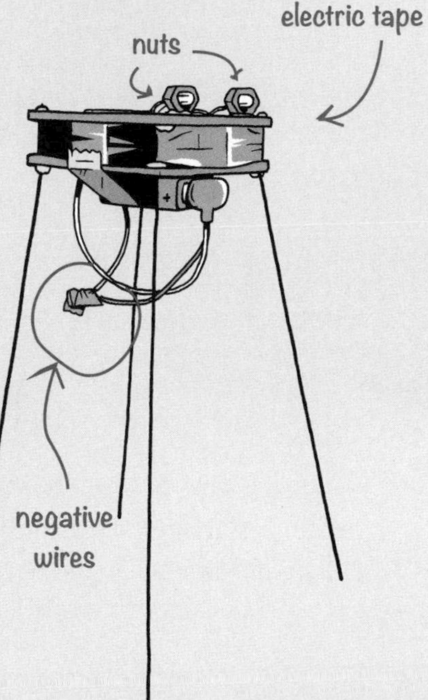

TESLA'S

DO-IT-YOURSELF SEMI-INVISIBLE BOTTLE BOT

THE STUFF

- 1 battery holder for 2 AAA batteries (A)
- 1 3-volt motor (available from most electronics stores; the RadioShack catalog number is 273-223) (B)
- 2 wire coat hangers
- 1 plastic 2-liter water bottle
- 2 plastic bottle caps
- 2 small metal washers
- 2 AAA batteries
- Hot-glue gun
- Wire cutters
- Pliers
- Scissors
- Duct tape
- Extra wire, nuts, bolts, and other spare pieces

A

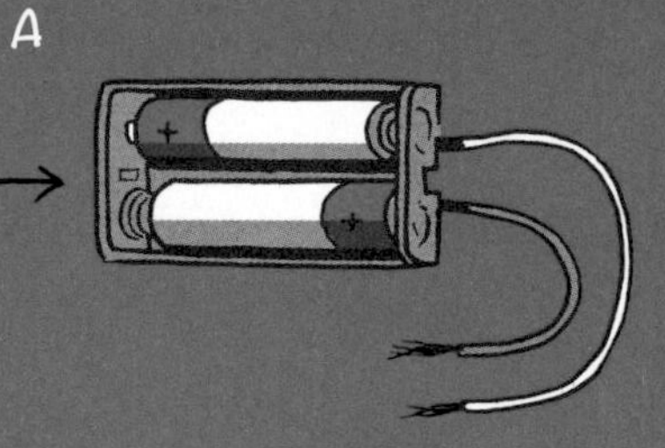

B

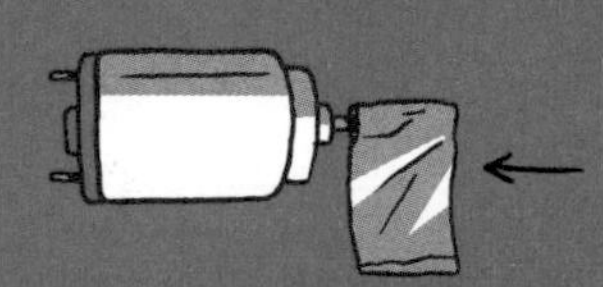

THE SETUP

1. Use the wire cutters to cut the hangers into sections about 14 inches (35.5 cm) long.
2. Use the pliers to bend each section of wire in the middle so that the curve of the wire matches the curve of the water bottle.
3. Adjust the bend so that each "leg" is even.
4. Bend the end of each wire to give your robot "feet."

1–4

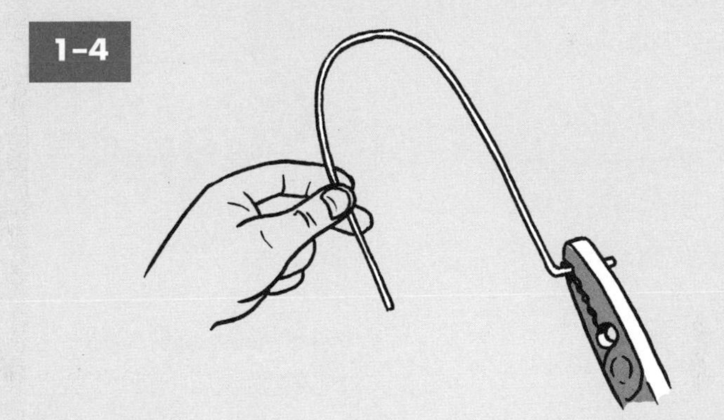

5. Test-fit the wire onto the bottle.
6. Hot-glue one wire onto the front of the bottle and the other onto the back.
7. Clip the wires if needed so that all four ends are the same length (this will help your robot stand on a flat surface).

8. Hot-glue the battery holder to the bottom of your robot so that the wires face toward the back of the bot.

9. Use scissors to cut a strip of duct tape about ½ inch (1.25 cm) long.

10. Fold the tape over the axle of the motor, making sure that the tape and axle spin freely.

11. Add another seven pieces of tape securely on top of the first. This will cause the motor to vibrate when it spins.

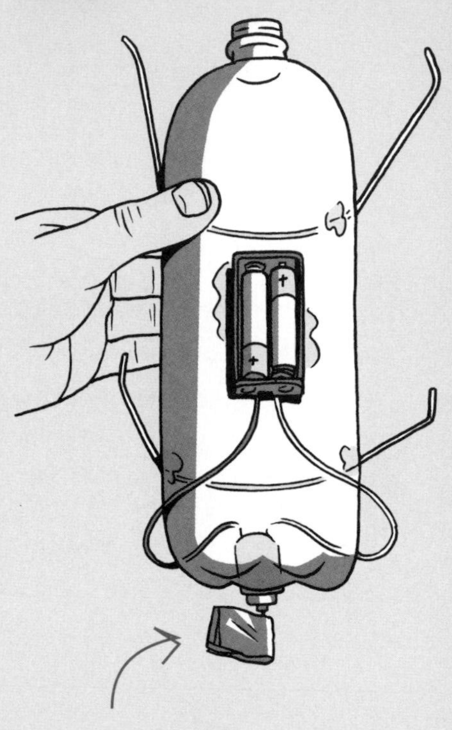

THE FINAL STEPS

1. Remove ¾ inch (2 cm) of the plastic from the ends of the battery holder wires and twist the wire onto one of the metal tabs of the motor. Repeat with the other wire and the other motor tab.

2. Hot-glue the motor onto the end of your robot, ensuring

that the tape can spin fully without hitting the bottle.

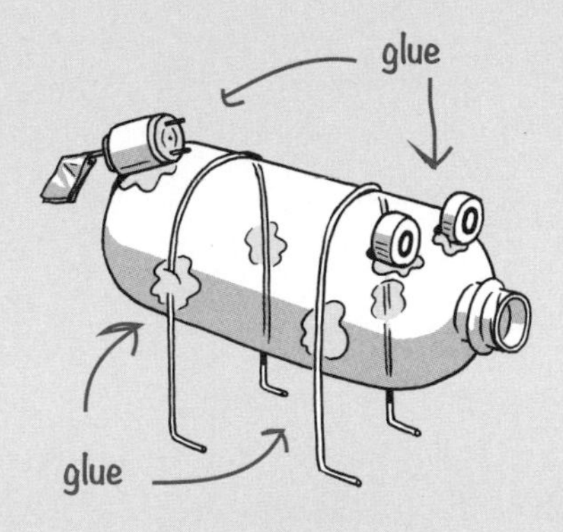

3. To make eyes, glue a small metal washer onto each bottle cap and then glue the caps onto the front of the robot.

4. Use lightweight wire, nuts, bolts and other roboty-looking pieces to decorate your bot. Filling the bottle with tangles of wire creates a nice colorful effect.

5. Add batteries, and the robot is ready to go! Tip: If your robot only goes backward, add some weight toward the front.

It took Nick and Tesla most of the day to figure out how their robots *should* work. The next morning, they took them onto the back porch to see if they *would* work. The basement lab would be too cramped if the robots moved the way they were supposed to. On top of that, the fresh, cool breeze off the ocean a quarter mile away would be a lot more pleasant than the heavy, smoky air in the basement, which still smelled like a five-alarm fire at a banana plantation.

Having their robo-showdown outside also gave Nick and Tesla an excuse to get away from their uncle, who'd been pestering them with questions they either couldn't answer or didn't want to.

"Do guys still bring gals boxes of chocolate, or is that just something I used to see in old cartoons?" Uncle Newt had asked.

Nick and Tesla shrugged.

"Is there such a thing as love at first sight, or is that simply a response to pheromones and stimulation of the medial prefrontal cortex triggered by subliminal visual cues?" Uncle Newt had asked.

Nick and Tesla shrugged again.

"Should I start working out?" Uncle Newt had asked, trying to flex an arm muscle and looking chagrined by the (non)result.

Nick and Tesla scooped up their robots and fled.

Unfortunately, although retreating to the back porch let them escape their uncle's questions, it put them square in the sights of his most unneighborly neighbor.

Julie Casserly was walking out to her car dressed for the gym in form-fitting red, blue, and white striped tights that made her look like a walking barber pole. She stopped in her driveway to glare at Nick and Tesla as they crouched over their creations.

"What are those?" she asked. "Time bombs?"

"No," said Tesla.

"Land mines?"

"No," said Tesla.

"Nuclear reactors?"

"They're just robots," said Nick (who usually tried to stay out of these conversations).

"Oh." Julie looked at her watch. "And when should I expect them to go berserk and begin attacking people?"

Tesla picked up her robot and showed it to her.

"Look. It's the size of a cat and it's made out of a soda bottle. You have nothing to worry about."

"Yeah. Sure. 'Nothing to worry about,'" Julie said. "Just make sure those things stay on your uncle's side of the property line. I don't want my lawn hurt when the explosions start."

She got in her car and drove off.

"I blame sci-fi," Tesla said.

"What?" said Nick.

"Science fiction. There's always robots on the rampage, trying to take over the world of whatever. It gives 'em a bad rap. They're really just cool tools that happen to move around on their own."

"Speaking of which," said Nick, "it's time to see who's gonna win that five million dollars."

(Nick and Tesla often made bets with each other for high stakes. When they'd come to live with Uncle Newt, Nick already owed Tesla $14 million. Now it was up to $21 million.)

"Right," Tesla said. "You do the countdown, then we'll let the Teslanator and Frank go head to head."

The Teslanator was Tesla's robot.

Nick, for some reason, had named his robot Frank.

They put down their robots so they were facing each other on the cracked cement of the porch.

"Three," said Nick. "Two . . . *one*."

Tesla pushed the Teslanator's batteries into place.

Nick twisted together the black and red wires on top of Frank.

Both robots came to life, hopping rapidly back and forth on their spindly little legs.

Tesla whooped and pumped her fist in the air. "Get him, Teslanator! Tear him apart!"

"Go, Frank!" cheered Nick. "Destroy! Destroy!"

The Teslanator and Frank wobbled forward into each other, then bounced away and began moving in

opposite directions.

"So they're not exactly battlebots," Nick said. "But they both work great."

"Yeah," said Tesla. "I think yours is a little faster, though."

"And I think yours looks cooler."

"Thanks. Tie?"

Tesla held out her hand.

Nick took it and shook.

"Tie," he said. "And thanks for the distraction. I needed it."

Yet Tesla could already see the sadness and worry creeping back into Nick's eyes, even as he watched Frank scuttle off toward the grass. She hadn't kept her brother's mind off their parents for long. What would her next distraction be?

The Teslanator bumped into the rusty ruins of an old barbecue grill and changed direction again. Now it was doing a quick, quivering walk up the concrete path to the driveway.

"Watch out!" Nick called to the robot. "It's a big, dangerous world out there!"

Tesla rolled her eyes. "Oh, don't listen to him, Teslanator. The world's big, but it's not dangerous. Roam! Discover! *Live!*"

The little robot seemed to scuttle away even faster, as if it heard Tesla's words and was anxious to enjoy its newfound freedom.

Then a bicycle zipped around the house and crushed it flat.

"No!" cried Tesla.

"Blurk!" cried Nick (who was always more thrown by surprises than his sister, something he attributed to the fact that he was twelve minutes younger than she).

"You've gotta come with me!" said the boy riding the bike: Nick and Tesla's friend DeMarco. "It's an—hey." He glanced down at the little robot he'd just flattened beneath his tires. "Did I run over a walking bottle of root beer?"

"Yes," Nick said.

"Oh. Sorry." DeMarco took in a deep breath and started again. "You've gotta come with me! It's an emergency!"

He wheeled his bike around and sped off.

Nick and Tesla ran around the house after him.

"What's going on?" Tesla called out.

"I told you!" DeMarco shouted over his shoulder. "It's an emergency!"

"What kind of emergency?" said Nick.

"The bad kind!"

Nick looked at Tesla. "Is there a good kind?"

DeMarco swooped out of the driveway and started pedaling up the street. He was addicted to adrenaline—he'd once told Nick and Tesla that when he grew up, he wanted to be a motocross driver, a stuntman, a mixed martial arts cage fighter, or, preferably, all three. But he didn't go looking for trouble or imagine it when it wasn't there. If he said there was an emergency, there was an emergency.

"Come on," said Tesla, running to the garage. "We'd better see what's wrong."

"I hope Silas is OK," said Nick.

Silas was another friend from the neighborhood. He and DeMarco were total opposites. DeMarco was small and quick and excitable and came from a large family. Silas was big and slow and mellow and an only child. Yet they were inseparable. As far as Nick and Tesla knew, they spent every waking moment together.

So where was Silas now?

There were two bicycles in the garage: a rusty old ten-speed and a like-new mountain bike Uncle Newt had picked up for the kids at a garage sale the week before. Nick hopped on the ten-speed, even though the gears were a complete mystery to him and he always felt like he was trying to pedal up Mount Everest even when they were riding downhill.

Tesla had bought the right to ride the mountain bike all summer for $4 million.

By the time she and Nick raced down the driveway, DeMarco was a block ahead of them. They followed him up the street, around the corner, and out of the neighborhood. He had to stop when he hit a red light at the Pacific Coast Highway, but before Nick and Tesla could catch up the light turned green and he went speeding into downtown Half Moon Bay.

"I think I know where we're going," said Tesla.

"Me . . . too," Nick panted as he pumped with all his might on the ten-speed. "But what kind of . . . emergency could there be . . . there?"

A minute later, Nick and Tesla saw that their guess was right. DeMarco was hopping off his bike outside the town's one and only comic-book shop—which Silas's family owned. Whenever Silas and DeMarco weren't cruising around on their bikes looking for something to do, they could be found there flipping through the latest issue of *Scorpion-Boy* or *The Unstoppable Captain Carnage*.

HERO WORSHIP, INCORPORATED, the sign over the door said. COMICS • COLLECTIBLES • STUFF YOUR MOM WOULD THROW AWAY (BUT SHOULDN'T).

Standing at attention beneath the sign, fists on his hips and feet spread apart, was a tall figure clad in blue-and-gold armor: a statue of the superhero Metalman. DeMarco paused a moment beside it, gesturing for Nick and Tesla to hurry up, before going inside. Nick and Tesla parked their bicycles in a nearby rack—both noting that Silas's bike was already there—and followed DeMarco into the store.

Hero Worship, Incorporated was like a smaller version of the old Wonder Hut—dark, grungy, and cramped. There were thousands of comics in long, thin boxes, and toys and trading cards and posters and DVDs were packed in everywhere, too. What *wasn't* packing the place were customers. This morning, like too many mornings, there were none.

Sitting behind the counter was a big, burly man with a thick black beard and a fondness for plaid flannel shirts and knit caps. It always seemed to Nick as though Paul Bunyan had put down his axe and opened up a comic-book shop.

Except it wasn't Paul Bunyan, of course. It was Silas's dad, Dave Kuskie. He was hunched over with his head in his hands.

Silas and DeMarco stood watching him with forlorn looks on their faces.

"We're ruined," Mr. Kuskie moaned. "*Ruined.*"

"Hi, guys," Silas said to Nick and Tesla. "Thanks for coming."

Mr. Kuskie jerked his head up in surprise. His eyes

were red and puffy, his round, usually friendly face pale.

He looked at Nick and Tesla, then DeMarco, and then finally Silas.

"Son," he said, shaking his head, "which part of 'Leave this to the grown-ups' did you not understand?"

"The part about leaving it to the grown-ups, I guess," Silas said.

He wasn't being sarcastic.

He also didn't understand rhetorical questions.

"Mr. Kuskie," DeMarco said, "if leaving it to grown-ups is gonna work, why do you keep sitting there saying, 'We're ruined, we're ruined'?"

"Well . . . because . . ." Silas's father buried his face in his hands again. "We're ruined."

Silas walked around the counter to pat him on the back. As he passed one of the store's jumble-covered shelves, a little silver shape on it came to life.

It was another robot, like the one Nick, Tesla, and Uncle Newt had seen inside Ranalli's Italian Kitchen. Only instead of wearing a chef's hat, it sported a cape and mask. And instead of spinning fake pizza dough, it raised a shiny finger and pointed it at Silas.

"Crime does not pay, evildoer," it croaked in a

droning voice, its rectangular plastic “mouth” flashing red with each syllable.

The “evildoer” ignored it.

“Come on, Dad,” Silas said. “Nick and Tesla are smart. They can help. Just like they helped that girl a couple weeks ago.”

Oh, man, Nick thought. *Rescue one kidnapped girl, and people start thinking you’re kid detectives.*

A chill ran through him, but he couldn’t tell if it was from excitement, pride, embarrassment, or dread.

“I don’t know if we can help, Mr. Kuskie,” Tesla

said. "But I do know that telling us what happened couldn't hurt."

Silas's dad lifted his head and gave her a skeptical look. It was clear *he* wasn't convinced they were kid detectives. Yet after a moment, he sighed and started talking.

"I had it in my hands. Right here in the store. The answer to all our problems . . . and now it's gone!" Mr. Kuskie leaned forward and pierced Nick and Tesla with a look of wide-eyed horror. "A mint-condition copy of *Stupefying* #6!"

There was a long, awkward silence as Mr. Kuskie waited for Nick and Tesla to react.

"So . . ." Nick said. "That's . . . a comic book?"

Mr. Kuskie looked appalled. "You don't know?"

Nick and Tesla shook their heads.

"Aren't you guys into comic books?" DeMarco asked them.

"Not really," Tesla said.

Nick waggled a hand. "Meh."

"But . . . but . . ." Silas spluttered. "You're nerds!"

"*What?*" Nick and Tesla said together.

"You do science projects for fun," Silas said, "and you read books—without pictures!—even when you don't have to. Obviously, you're nerds. And all nerds love comics . . . don't they?"

"No," Tesla said. "They do not."

"Not that it matters," Nick threw in. "Because it doesn't apply to us. We're not nerds."

He turned and gave his sister an uncertain look that silently added, "Or are we?"

She was looking at Silas's dad.

"So this *Stupefying* #6," she said, "it's valuable?"

Mr. Kuskie nodded solemnly. "*Stupefying Comics* #6 from July of 1944 features the first-ever appearance of a certain special someone named Metalman. You do know Metalman, don't you?"

"Of course," said Nick. "We've even seen the movies."

Mr. Kuskie nodded again. "Sure you have. Metalman is one of the most popular superheroes in the world. Which means *Stupefying* #6 isn't just valuable. It's very, very, very, very, *very* valuable."

"How did you get a copy?" Tesla asked.

"I found it at an estate sale yesterday morning."

Tesla furrowed her brow. "Estate sale?"

"If you die," Silas explained, "and, like, there's no one you wanted to give your stuff to, then, like, it's all sold off one day to whoever walks into your house and pays for it."

"Sounds like the Yard Sale of the Dead," Tesla said.

Nick shivered. "Creepy."

"Not really," said Mr. Kuskie. "You can find amazing stuff at estate sales. And if someone doesn't buy something, it just gets hauled off to the dump. That's probably what would've happened to that copy of *Stupefying* #6 if I hadn't found it. It was at the bottom of a big pile of old *Life* magazines and issues of *Reader's Digest* and junk comics that aren't worth a nickel. Whoever had it all these years had no idea it was valuable. But I knew. And that Barry Dobek—he knew, too."

For the first time, Nick saw something like spite on Mr. Kuskie's face.

"Who's Barry Dobek?" Tesla asked.

"He owns one of the antiques places up the street. The Treasure Trove," Mr. Kuskie said. "He hits the local estate sales every weekend, too. Always tries to beat me to any good comics or toys, even though that's not his business at all. He just likes competition . . . and winning. When he saw me with *Stupefying* #6, I thought his head was going to explode."

"I see," Tesla said, nodding knowingly. "And after you bought the comic, you brought it to the store?"

"Yeah. I put it in a manila envelope and left it right there." Mr. Kuskie waved a hand at a sloppy stack of comic books and magazines piled on the floor behind the counter. "I was going to put it in a safety-deposit box this morning and then set up an online auction. This isn't the kind of comic you sell to any schmo who walks in off the street. I was going to make enough from it to pay off all our debts and make sure the bank doesn't—"

Mr. Kuskie cut himself off, his gaze drifting to half a dozen white envelopes piled up by the cash register.

They looked like bills.

"The store hasn't been doing well," Mr. Kuskie said sheepishly.

"We noticed" was the first response that occurred to Nick. He thought it best not to say it.

"So what happened to the comic book?" Tesla asked.

"I don't know," Mr. Kuskie said with a shrug. "When I came in this morning, it just . . . wasn't here."

Tesla opened her mouth.

"And before you ask," Mr. Kuskie said, "*no*. I did not simply lose it. You don't misplace a miracle when it drops into your lap."

"You've gone to the police, then?" Tesla asked.

Mr. Kuskie nodded, but the way he tilted his head and pinched his lips and *almost* rolled his eyes made it obvious he didn't think much would come of a call to Half Moon Bay's police force.

The "force" was composed entirely of one overworked cop and one elderly clerk.

"Sgt. Feiffer came and looked the place over," Mr. Kuskie said, "but he couldn't find any evidence of a break-in."

"So how did the thief get inside?" Tesla said.

"I have no idea! The doors were still locked when I came in this morning."

"Who has keys?" Tesla asked.

"Just me, though there's a spare set that I . . ." Mr. Kuskie tilted his head farther to the side, looking even more skeptical than before. "Explain to me again why I'm telling this to a couple of twelve-year-olds."

"We're eleven, actually," Nick said.

It was his first contribution to the investigation.

Tesla threw him a glare that told him what she

thought of it.

"So," she said, turning back to Silas's dad, "who else knew you had the comic book?"

Mr. Kuskie just looked at her for a moment and then shook his head sadly.

"You know what? This is ridiculous. Metalman's not going to save the store, and neither is Nancy Drew. I appreciate your willingness to help, but I'd prefer it if you'd just leave." He turned to his son. "Silas. Please."

"All right, Dad. Let's go, guys."

Silas began ushering his friends toward the door.

"Now where was I?" Nick heard Mr. Kuskie mutter as they stepped outside. "Oh, yeah. *I'm ruined*."

"I overheard him talking to Sgt. Feiffer," Silas said once the kids were outdoors beside Metalman. "He really might have to close Hero Worship for good. I had no idea we were going broke, but . . . well, I guess we are. That comic book was going to save the store. Now that it's gone . . ."

Silas shrugged miserably.

Nick placed a hand on one of his friend's broad, slumping shoulders. "I'm sorry, Silas."

"Can't you guys call in that spy lady with your little dog collars?" DeMarco said to Nick and Tesla. "I bet she could help."

"It doesn't work like that," Tesla told him.

"That spy lady" was Agent McIntyre, a friend of their parents who'd helped get them out of trouble once before. She tracked Nick and Tesla, they suspected, with star-shaped pendants their mom and dad had given to them—the "little dog collars."

Tesla pulled out hers from under her shirt—she and Nick never went anywhere without them—and spoke into it.

"Calling Agent McIntyre. Calling Agent McIntyre. Missing comic book alert! I repeat, missing comic book alert! Respond, please."

Tesla pressed the pendant to her ear, shook it, pressed it to her ear again, then stuffed it back under her shirt.

"Nothing," she said.

"All right. Geez," DeMarco grumbled. "You don't have to get all snarky about it. I just thought Agent McIntyre could help us."

“Who says we need her help?” said Tesla. She turned to Silas. “You say you heard what your dad told Sgt. Feiffer?”

Silas nodded.

“*Everything* he told Feiffer?” Tesla said.

Silas nodded again.

Tesla crossed her arms and narrowed her eyes. “Perfect,” she said. “Then tell *us*.”

There were two sets of keys to the store, Silas said. One Mr. Kuskie kept with him at all times. The backup he hid in the Metalman statue. Stick your finger in Metalman’s right ear, and the keys would pop out of the left.

“You’re kidding,” Tesla said.

Silas shook his head gravely. “The keys used to be in his nose, but people kept picking it.”

“All right,” Tesla said with a dismissive wave of the hand. “Go on.”

“Well . . . I guess they just thought it was funny. And it was, actually. You could get your fingers waaaaaaaaaaay up there, and sometimes people would stick their gum in his—"

"I meant go on *about the robbery*," Tesla said.

"Oh. Right."

The spare keys, Silas reported, were still in Metalman's ear after the robbery. And the only people who knew about them were Mr. Kuskie, Mrs. Kuskie, and—because he was sometimes allowed to open the store if his father was running late—Silas.

Not many people knew about *Stupefying* #6, either. Besides Silas, the only people who knew Mr. Kuskie had the comic book were the stranger he'd bought it from at the estate sale—a woman who'd barely glanced up from the romance novel she'd been reading long enough to give Mr. Kuskie his change—and Barry Dobek, the jerky antiques store guy. The lady obviously had no idea (or interest in) who Mr. Kuskie was, and Dobek couldn't have known where he'd hidden the comic. Yet there was no sign the store had been searched. The thief had known exactly where to go.

And finally, Mr. Kuskie had been so upset when he discovered that the comic was gone that he went to the little bathroom in the back of the store and started to barf. But all he'd had for breakfast was a chocolate doughnut hole and a cup of coffee, so—

"That's enough, Silas!" Tesla said.

"You told me to tell you everything."

"Yeah, well—we've got what we need."

"What we need to do what?" Nick asked.

He already knew the answer, though.

It was obvious Silas and DeMarco weren't the only ones who now thought that Tesla and Nick were kid detectives.

"We're going to get that comic book back and save the store, of course," Tesla said. "And I know just where to start."

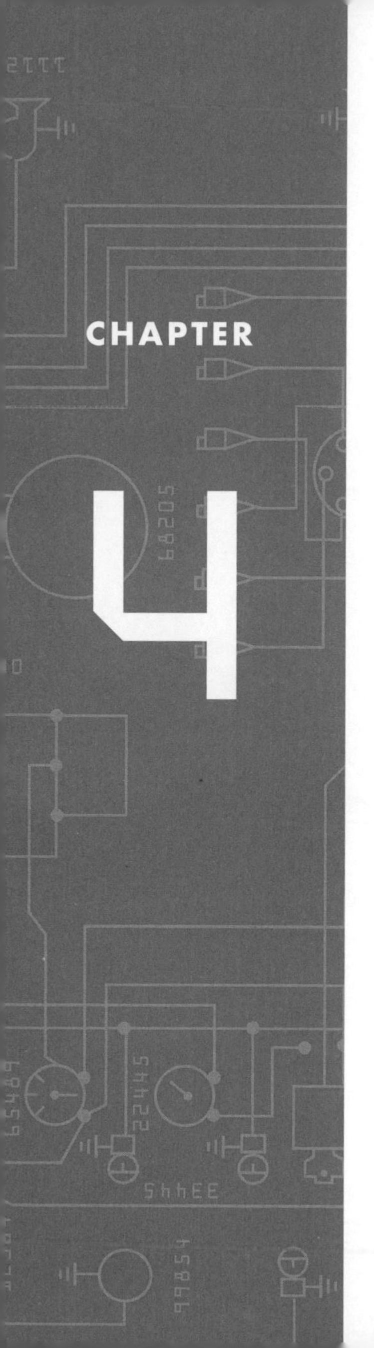

CHAPTER 4

The place to start, apparently, was the It's-Froze-Yo! self-serve yogurt shop up the street. Tesla led Nick, Silas, and DeMarco there, then stood looking inside as customers filled their bowls with nice, healthy, fruit-based frozen yogurts . . . which they promptly buried under gummy worms, crumbled candy bars, and chocolate sauce.

"Sorry, Tesla," Silas said, "but I'm not really in the mood for dessert right now."

"We're not here for dessert," Tesla said. "Take a peek across the street." The boys all turned to look.

Directly across from It's-Froze-Yo! was a wine shop and an art gallery. And above them: the Treasure Trove, Barry Dobek's antiques store. It was a bright, warm summer day, and the store's windows were open. Beyond them, Nick could see lampshades and chandeliers and slow-spinning fans hanging from the ceiling.

A lanky, gray-haired man with a pair of glasses pushed up onto the top of his head appeared near one of the open windows, gesturing at something Nick couldn't see, while a pop-eyed woman beside him nodded excitedly.

"Silas," Tesla said, "describe Dobek."

She was still staring into the frozen yogurt store. In fact, some of the customers had begun to notice her and were staring back.

"I don't need to describe Dobek," Silas said. "Just turn around and you'll see him."

He started to lift an arm toward the man with the glasses.

Tesla grabbed the arm and pushed it down.

"*Don't point*," she growled. "And turn around, would you? I said take a peek, not stare until Dobek notices you."

The boys turned toward It's-Froze-Yo!—and found themselves facing a family of four that was trying to enjoy some yogurt while being watched like a bunch of monkeys at the zoo.

Nick looked over their heads and pretended he was giving serious consideration to the list of the day's flavors posted on the wall.

"Silas, does Dobek know who you are?" Tesla said.

"Yeah. I go with my dad to the estate sales sometimes, so I've met him."

"Which means there's a good chance he knows DeMarco's a friend of yours, since you two are like a couple of conjoined twins."

"I guess so," Silas said.

"Hey!" DeMarco protested.

"Can we go stare at something else, please?" said Nick. A bitter-looking teenage girl behind the cash register had started shooting him nasty looks.

"Dobek doesn't know me and Nick, though," Tesla mused, ignoring her brother. "That gives us an opportunity."

"What opportunity?" Nick said, his voice quavering.

The register girl was stomping toward them.

"Ooo," Silas said when he noticed her. "What crawled up *her* nose?"

"Us," Nick said.

The girl jerked open the store's front door, leaned out, and snarled, "Do you want some of this frozen glop, or are you just going to stand there freaking out the people who do?"

Tesla gave her a smile. "No glop for us, thanks."

She took Nick by the arm and began dragging him away, headed for the nearest street corner.

"My brother and I are going antiquing," she said.

"I think you need to slow down, Tez," Nick said as he and his sister crossed the street.

"Slow down?" Tesla jerked her head at an SUV that was inching toward them, the driver obviously begrudging them the four seconds it would take to get from one side of Main Street to the other. "Does this look like a good time to slow down?"

"I'm not talking about how fast you're walking

I'm talking about how you're running off to play detective."

Tesla stopped and whirled to face her brother. Fortunately, they were out of the street by then.

"I'm not 'running off to play detective.' I'm just trying to help a friend. If someone doesn't get that comic book back, Silas's family is going to lose their store. No store, no money. No money, no *food*. The Kuskies might have to become migrant field hands or move to Alaska to work on fishing boats or sell their kidneys to sick billionaires or something."

"Sell their kidneys to sick billionaires? Don't you think that's laying it on a bit thick?"

"Maybe. But tell me this: if we don't find that comic book, who will?"

"How about the people whose job it is? The police."

"Half Moon Bay's finest? Remind me, Nick, what was Sgt. Feiffer doing the last time we saw him?"

Nick rubbed his chin. "Let me see. He waaaaaaas . . . oh. Now I remember."

They'd last crossed paths with Sgt. Feiffer three days before. He was chasing an unlicensed dog that was chasing the Newtmobile.

Not only could Half Moon Bay not afford a police

force anymore, it couldn't afford an animal control officer, either.

"And the time before that?" Tesla said.

Nick thought it over.

Five days before, they'd seen Sgt. Feiffer giving a ticket to a very unhappy-looking ice-cream truck driver who'd been selling his popsicles and orange Push Ups too close to a fire hydrant.

Half Moon Bay couldn't pay for meter officers anymore either.

"All right," he said. "You win."

Even if Sgt. Feiffer had been a brilliant detective—and Nick had no way of knowing if he was—he'd probably be too busy cornering rabid chipmunks and ticketing double-parked cars to track down a comic-book thief.

"So we go into Dobek's antiques store," Nick said, "and then what?"

"I have no idea," Tesla said, starting toward the Treasure Trove again.

After a few quick steps, she turned and flashed her brother a grin.

"Maybe I *am* going too fast," she said.

Yet she didn't slow down.

Mr. Kuskie had been right when he'd said the Treasure Trove didn't sell the kinds of things you'd find at Hero Worship, Incorporated. To catch Barry Dobek's eye, it seemed, something had to be not just old but musty and dusty and dark and *dull*.

The Treasure Trove was filled with furniture mostly, though there were also some "vintage" (a.k.a. moth-eaten) clothes and display cases stocked with costume jewelry and cuff links and spectacles and shaving kits and other stuff that generally made Tesla feel like she needed a nap. The one kid-friendly thing in the place was a barrel of candy. Except the candy was salt-water taffy the color of slugs, and Tesla wouldn't have paid a penny for the whole barrel, let alone the quarter per piece that Dobek was charging.

Dobek seemed as drab and lifeless as his store. He was a tall, thin, gray man with a long, bony face and white hair he swept straight back into a pompadour. He was dressed casually, in jeans and a denim shirt, yet the clothes looked so spotless and stiff—so unlived in—he may as well have been in a freshly pressed business suit. His glasses were still pushed up on top of his head, as if they weren't glasses at all but a strange kind of hat worn purely for decoration.

At first, he ignored Tesla and Nick as they moved slowly up and down the aisles. He obviously preferred to focus on the adults in the store, which made a certain sense. How many kids are going to shell out $1,000 for an eighteenth-century *buffet deux corps*? (Tesla had no idea what an "eighteenth-century *buffet deux corps*" was until she saw the words written on the price tag. To her, it just looked like a dinged-up old cabinet.)

Eventually, a couple to whom Dobek had been trying to sell a "petite English oak barley-twist drop-leaf wine table" (whatever that was) beat a hasty retreat, and Nick and Tesla were the only customers left in the store.

"He's looking at us," Nick whispered as he and Tesla pretended to examine a collection of antique chamber pots.

Tesla tried to steal a casual look at Dobek.

He was near the front of the store, looking back at her in a way that didn't seem casual at all. It seemed pretty serious, in fact.

Dobek was frowning and furrowing his bushy white eyebrows.

Tesla turned her back to him again.

"Just act natural," she said under her breath.

"How should I know what 'natural' is in a place like this?"

"Do what the grown-ups did. Stare at boring old junk, nod like you know what you're looking at, and if Dobek asks if you need any help, say, 'Just looking.'"

Nick tried staring at boring old junk and nodding like he knew what he was looking at.

"He's still watching us," he muttered after all of five seconds. "What are we doing in here, anyway?"

"Watching and waiting," Tesla said.

"Watching and waiting for what?"

"I have no idea, remember?"

Nick threw his sister a glare.

"You know, Tez," he said, "sometimes your plans leave something to be desired. Like *a plan*."

Tesla just smiled and shrugged, though she was starting to worry that they were indeed wasting their time. If hanging out around the Treasure Trove didn't result in any leads, she wasn't sure what to do next. Yet she was determined to continue the hunt for the missing comic. And not just for the sake of Silas and his dad and Hero Worship, Incorporated.

Nick needed a distraction. It had been fun messing around in Uncle Newt's basement lab—Nick and Tesla had always loved gadgets and gizmos and science. But day by day, Tesla had watched her brother's excitement fade and his worry grow.

Why hadn't their parents called? And what were they *really* doing in Uzbekistan—if that was truly where they were?

Tesla was as much in the dark as her brother. So she would give him different questions to wrestle with instead.

Who'd taken *Stupefying Comics #6*?

How had they known where it was hidden?

Why were there no signs of a break-in?

And why was Barry Dobek suddenly looming over them with a scowl on his face?

Tesla jumped.

That last question had caught her by surprise. Her brother, too.

"Justlookingjustlooking!" Nick blurted out.

Dobek leaned in toward him.

"Oh, I know you are," he sneered. "I know what you're looking *for*, too . . . and you're not going to get it!"

CHAPTER 5

Dobek spread his feet apart and put his hands on his hips. It made him look a bit like the Metalman statue outside Hero Worship, Incorporated—and he seemed just as immovable.

To Tesla it seemed as if he was planting himself between her and Nick and the exit, making himself an obstacle they couldn't get around.

Trapping them.

"If you'd moved a little quicker, you might have gotten away with it," Dobek said. "But you dawdled, and now you've lost your chance."

Nick opened his mouth.

"Uhh," he said.

He swallowed hard, then tried again.

All that come out was another "uhh."

"Lost our chance for *what?*" Tesla said.

Dobek smirked down at her. "Please. I'm not a fool. I don't have toys or games. There's only one thing in this whole place that would interest anyone under the age of eighteen. And whenever I see children in here who weren't dragged in by their parents, I know that's what they're after."

He threw a meaningful glance at the nearby barrel of salt-water taffy.

"And if they don't pay for some and leave within a minute," Dobek went on, "I know they're not planning on paying at all."

Tesla was so annoyed to be lumped in with "children"—she and Nick were nearly twelve!—it took her a moment to realize what Dobek was saying.

When she did, she started laughing.

"You thought we were going to steal taffy? Really? I hate that stuff!"

Nick let out a laugh, too—a shrill cackle of nervous relief.

"Yeah, salt-water taffy's the worst!" he said. "Not

only would I not steal it, you couldn't pay me to eat it. It's like chewing on someone's old gym shoes!"

Nick laughed again.

Dobek narrowed his eyes and flared his nostrils.

Nick stopped laughing.

"Sorry," he mumbled.

"So," Dobek said, "why are you here, then? And don't tell me you're looking for a rococo chaise longue because it would be just the thing to tie the living room together."

"Well . . ." said Tesla.

She had no idea what was going to come out of her mouth next.

"We're waiting for our parents," said Nick.

Dobek arched an eyebrow at him.

Tesla almost did, too.

"Ohhh?" Dobek said.

Nick nodded sadly. "They ran off to do some stupid grown-up thing, and we're just supposed to hang around in limbo until they come back . . . whenever that'll be."

For a moment, Dobek almost—*almost*—looked sympathetic. But the moment passed quickly.

"That doesn't answer my question," he said.

"Why are you in *here?*"

"Well . . ." said Nick, "you see . . ."

His eyes met Tesla's and flashed a quick S.O.S.

"Our parents are in the gallery downstairs," Tesla said. "Picking out art for our new beach house."

"Ohhh?" Dobek said again. But it was different than his earlier "Ohhh?" It was about an octave higher and it was said with widened eyes and the beginnings of a smile.

Tesla nodded. "Mom can't stand bare walls, even for a few days. So she's making Dad buy half the stuff in the gallery. When they're done, they're coming up here to look for furniture."

Dobek switched from "Ohhh?" to "Ahhh." A very happy "Ahhh."

"Well, they're coming to the right place," he said. "The Treasure Trove has the best selection of antique furniture between Monterey and San Francisco."

"We can see that," Tesla said. "Right, Herbert?"

It took Nick a moment to realize *he* was Herbert.

"Oh, yeah," he said to Dobek. "Gertrude's right. Mom and Dad are gonna love this place."

Gertrude—a.k.a. Tesla—had to fight the urge to kick her brother in the shin. She hadn't meant anything by calling him "Herbert." The name had just popped into her head, maybe because it felt as old-timey as everything in the Treasure Trove. But "Gertrude" was really pushing it.

Dobek didn't seem to notice, though.

"Excellent. *Excellent*," he said with a simpering smile. "I hope you'll forgive me for coming on a bit strong a moment ago. Half Moon Bay is a lovely community—you're going to just love it here!—but we do have a few little hooligans running around."

"We understand," said Tesla.

"I think we've seen some already," Nick added. "There were these weird kids staring at us when we stopped for frozen yogurt . . ."

Now Tesla *really* wanted to kick her brother in the shin. Or at least slap a hand over his mouth.

Somehow, she resisted.

"Allrighty then," Dobek said. "I'm looking forward to meeting your parents. While you're waiting for them, feel free to help yourselves to—"

He started to gesture toward the barrel of taffy, then caught himself, his smile wavering.

"A good look around," he said.

"Thanks," said Nick.

"We'll do that," said Tesla.

Dobek nodded and clasped his hands together—he was practically bowing—then finally turned his back to them and walked away.

"'Gertrude'?" Tesla growled at Nick.

"'Herbert'?" he growled back.

Tesla had a comeback ready—"If the name fits, *Herb* . . ."—but she gritted her teeth and swallowed it down.

It kind of blows your cover if you get into an argument about your aliases.

"Anyway," Tesla said, "good save with the waiting-for-the-parents bit."

Nick shrugged listlessly. "Guess it was already on my mind."

Tesla stole a glance at Dobek. He'd settled himself on a stool behind the counter.

Noticing that Tesla was looking his way, he gave her a little wave.

Tesla waved back, then tried to look fascinated by a set of rickety-looking dining room chairs.

"How much longer are we going to keep doing this?" Nick asked.

As long as it takes for this not to have been a complete

waste of time, Tesla thought. What she said was, "Long enough." Which meant more or less the same thing but didn't sound so pessimistic.

Dobek sat at the counter looking pleasantly attentive for a while. But when it became clear that Herbert and Gertrude's parents weren't going to pop in right away, credit cards at the ready, he pulled down the glasses atop his head, perched them on the end of his nose, and went back to reading a book he'd left sitting by the cash register.

The book was called *Entomophobia and You: Stop Buggin' about Bugs!*

Tesla elbowed her brother and jerked her head at the book.

Nick glowered at her, peeked back, then mouthed the words *So what?*

That was when the phone rang.

"The Treasure Trove, Barry Dobek speaking. Ahh, Anton! What perfect timing. *I got it.*"

Tesla and Nick froze.

"It wasn't easy, but it was worth it," Dobek went on. "I think you're going to be very, very pleased. It's in excellent condition."

Tesla fought the urge to turn and stare.

Nick apparently lost the same fight, because he *was* starting to turn.

Tesla jerked him around again.

"Hey, Herbert," she said a little too loudly. She pointed at a bulky piece of wood-and-glass furniture that looked like a cross between a cabinet and a transparent refrigerator. "Look at this . . . item."

"Oh, yeah," Nick said. "It'd be perfect for . . . uhhh . . . that place. With the stuff. By the thing."

Nick and Tesla stood there side by side, admiring the whatever-it-was that would go so well by the thing in the place with the stuff while Dobek chattered away behind them.

"We can talk price once you've seen it with your own eyes. Um-hmm. Yes. Exactly. I've got it right here with me."

There was a sharp *tap-tap*.

Dobek had rapped his knuckles on the countertop.

"When can you come in to take a look? Five it is. It's always slow around then anyway, and we'll want some privacy, won't we? To haggle." Dobek coughed out a little lifeless laugh. "Fine. I'll see you then."

Dobek hung up.

“Come on,” Tesla whispered to her brother. “We got what we came for.”

Nick nodded, and they headed for the door.

“Going so soon?” Dobek said when he noticed they were about to leave. He looked profoundly disappointed.

“We’re gonna see what’s holding up Mom and Dad,” Tesla said.

“They might have changed their minds and decided to go shopping for jewelry or a boat instead,” said Nick. “They’re like that.”

“Well, be sure and bring them back here if they still want furniture!”

“Oh, we’ll be back,” Tesla said as they headed out the door. “You can count on it.”

Tesla wasn’t sure if Silas and DeMarco would still be waiting outside the Treasure Trove when they came down the stairs. DeMarco had a hard time staying in one place for long, and when he drifted off looking for fun, Silas usually drifted with him.

Both boys were still across the street, though,

sitting on the pavement just outside It's-Froze-Yo! Tesla was impressed with their patience and commitment . . . until she realized that they hadn't even noticed her and Nick. They were too busy reading their comic books and eating their frozen yogurts.

So much for patience and commitment.

Tesla and Nick crossed the street and walked past the boys.

"Meet us around the corner," Tesla said without looking over at them.

"Huh?" said Silas. "Hey, wait up!"

Tesla heard DeMarco shush him.

"We don't want Dobek to see us together, remember?"

"Oh," said Silas. "Right."

Nick and Tesla just kept walking. When they reached the next corner, they turned and left Main Street behind.

A moment later, Silas and DeMarco came strolling around the corner with their hands in their pockets, their comics tucked under their arms, and dopey grins on their faces.

"Why are you smiling like that?" Tesla asked.

"We're trying to look inoculated," Silas said.

“I think you mean ‘innocuous,’” Tesla said. “And it’s not working.”

Silas and DeMarco pulled their hands out of their pockets, their grins melting.

“We think Dobek has the comic,” Nick said.

Silas and DeMarco perked up again.

“I knew it!” Silas said. “That jerk!”

“Why do you think Dobek’s got it?” said DeMarco.

“We heard him talking on the phone to someone named Anton,” Tesla said. “Sounded like a big-time collector. Dobek told him he’d gotten something for him, in good condition, but it wasn’t easy. Anton’s coming to the store at five to look it over.”

“That *jerk*!” Silas said again.

“We’ve gotta tell Sgt. Feiffer,” said DeMarco.

Tesla shook her head. “What would we tell him? We were eavesdropping on Dobek and *maybe* we heard him talking to someone who *might* be buying *Stupefying* #6 from him? It’s not enough. Sgt. Feiffer can’t just go barging into the Treasure Trove. He’d need a . . . a . . . a whatchamacallit.”

“Tank?” Silas guessed.

“Search warrant,” said Nick.

“Yeah. That,” Tesla said with a jerk of the head at

her brother. "Who knows how long it would take him to get one . . . if he could get one at all before Dobek got rid of the comic book."

"So what do we do?" DeMarco asked.

"We go back," Tesla said, "and we see whatever Dobek's got before this Anton does."

"And how are we going to do that?" asked Nick.

Tesla shrugged. "We need some kind of distraction. Something that gets Dobek away from the front counter. I got the feeling that's where he's keeping the comic book."

"That *jerk*!" Silas said yet again. For variety's sake, this time he drove a fist into his palm.

Tesla ignored him.

"It's too bad none of us has a pet roach," she said.

DeMarco gaped at her. "A pet *roach*?"

Tesla nodded. "Dobek's entomophobic."

"Thanks for clearing that up," DeMarco said, looking just as confused as before.

"He has a fear of insects," Nick explained. "We saw him reading a book about it."

"Ohhhh. Interesting," DeMarco said. "If I knew where to get a big bagful of bugs, I'd tell you."

"Why don't you just make some?" said Silas.

Tesla had gotten so used to ignoring him she barely even heard his words. She just stared off over his head, wondering about big bagfuls of bugs and where she could get one in a hurry.

Nick was listening, though.

"What do you mean?" he asked Silas.

"Oh, you know. You're always whipping up weird stuff down in your uncle's basement. Why not a bunch of bugs?"

Nick mulled that over, then turned to his sister. "Yeah . . . why *not* make our own bugs, Tez?"

Tesla looked at him to see if he was joking.

He wasn't.

After she'd thought about that a moment, she understood why.

A smile spread across her face, and she turned and said four words she thought she'd never say.

"Silas, you're a genius!"

NICK AND TESLA'S (AND SILAS'S, SORT OF)

HOMEMADE ROBO-BUG

THE STUFF

- 1 new toothbrush
- 1 paper clip
- 1 3V micro-vibration motor (available at most electronics stores; the RadioShack catalog number is 273-107) (A)
- 1 CR2032 3-volt button battery (B)
- 2 3-volt LED bulbs (C)
- Hot-glue gun
- Wire clippers
- Scissors

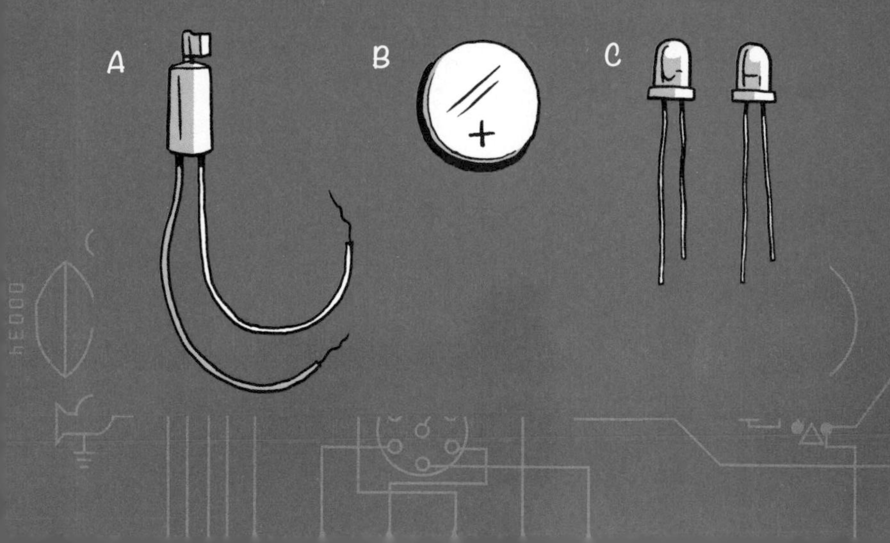

THE SETUP

1. Use the scissors to cut the toothbrush bristles to an equal length (if necessary).

2. Snip the head off the toothbrush with the wire clippers.

3. Trim the motor's wires so that they're about 3 inches (7.5 cm) long. (Set aside the extra piece of leftover black wire for later.) Remove the plastic coating from the last ¾ inch of each, exposing the wire.

4. Note that the LED bulbs have a longer wire and a shorter wire. Carefully twist together the two shorter wires of each LED bulb.

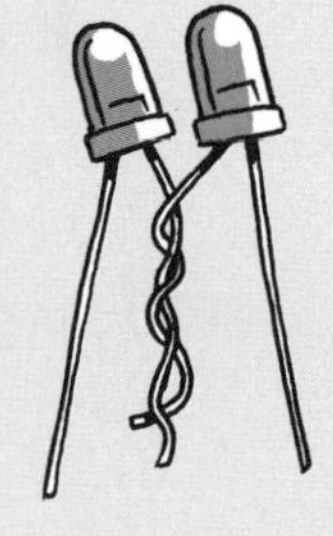

5. Tape the two loose LED wires *and* the red wire of the motor to the positive side of the battery (labeled +).

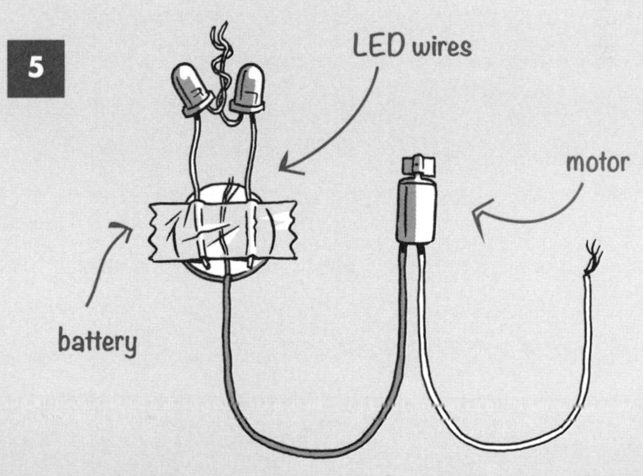

6. Straighten the paper clip.

7. Apply hot glue to the top of the toothbrush and attach the center of the paper clip to it.

8. Hot-glue the taped side of the battery to the top of the toothbrush, too.

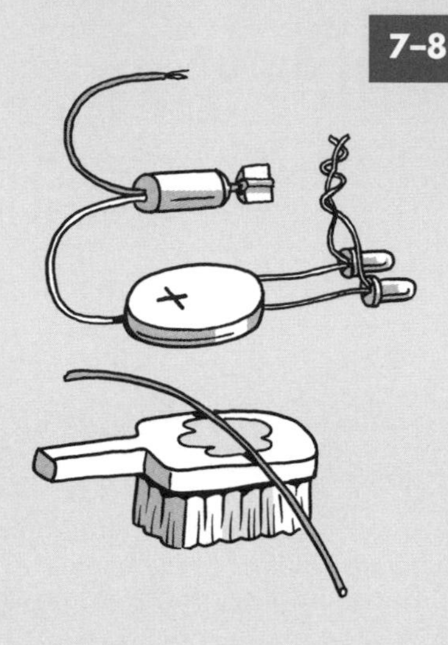

THE FINAL STEPS

1. Get the extra piece of black wire you cut from the motor. Expose the wire at each end and tape one end to the top of the battery.

2. Hot-glue the motor onto the top of the battery, with the spinner (the little spinning thingie on one end that gives the motor its bounce) in the front. Make sure the glue and wires don't prevent the spinner from spinning.

3. Bend down the ends of the paper clip so they almost touch the ground, as shown in the image of the completed robot on page 93. (The paper clip keeps your robot from tipping over.)

4. Connect the two black wires to the LED "antenna" wires.
5. Watch in amazement (or disgust, if you're entomophobic) as your robo-bug starts scurrying around just like the real thing—only with super-cool light-up eyes!

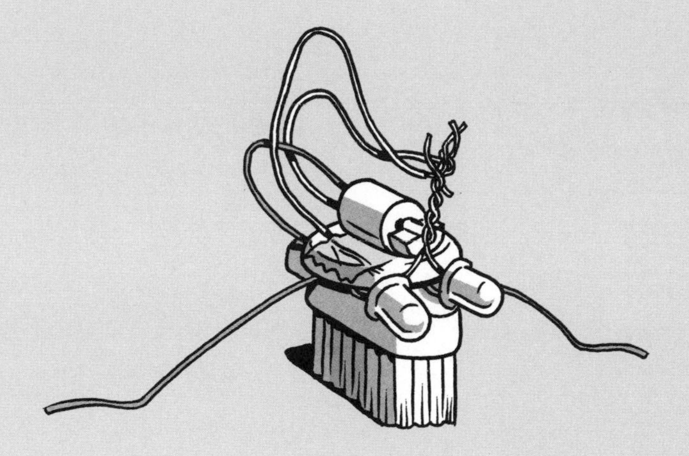

CHAPTER 6

Tesla could picture the robo-bug so clearly it was as if step-by-step instructions were floating in the air in front of her.

She assumed that she and Nick could build it, of course. She assumed that they could do anything until life proved otherwise (as it sometimes did).

But Tesla could think of only one kind of motor that would be small enough to run the little robot. And there was only one place in town where they might—*might*—be able to find one.

Nick knew it, too.

"The Wonder Hut?" he said.

"The Wonder Hut," said Tesla.

They started back toward Main Street. Silas and DeMarco fell in behind them.

"So you *are* gonna make your own bugs?" Silas asked.

"We're going to try," said Nick.

"Cool!"

Silas thought it over for a moment, then seemed to decide it wasn't so cool after all.

"Remind me again," he said. "How is a fake bug gonna get *Stupefying* #6 back for my dad?"

"One thing at a time, Silas," Tesla said. "One thing at a time."

She picked up her pace, as if her friend's question was something she wanted to leave behind.

When the kids got to the Wonder Hut, they found Duncan, the stocky little man who was usually hunched behind the counter reading, on his feet for once.

He was leaning against a spinner rack stocked

with dollhouse furniture while Curiosity the robot scratched his back.

"Oh, yeah," he moaned. "That's the spot."

He jumped when he noticed he was being watched, fumbling the rover's remote control so badly that Nick was afraid it was going to fly out of his hands.

Fortunately, Duncan managed to get a grip on the control box before it could hit the floor and burst into a thousand pieces.

"I had a horrible itch," the man said with a nervous laugh. "Right between my shoulder blades where I couldn't reach it."

He scurried around the counter and took up his usual position near the cash register.

"How can I help you today?"

You could go down the street and steal back a comic book for us, Nick thought.

"Did those new parts come in that you were expecting?" he asked.

"What are you looking for?"

"Mini-vibration motors."

Duncan jerked his flabby chin to the right. "Last aisle, halfway down, on the left. Between the motor-speed adjuster controller drivers and the ultrasonic distance sensors."

"Thanks," Nick said.

He started to walk away. But Tesla had already hurried off ahead of him, DeMarco and Silas on her heels. ("It's between the what and the what?" Silas was saying.) His sister would know what to look for. There was no reason Nick couldn't linger a moment over something that had caught his eye: Curiosity's control box. Duncan had left it on the counter.

Without even realizing he was doing it, Nick began reaching out a hand toward it.

"Do you think maybe I could try—?"

"No," Duncan snapped.

Nick jerked his hand back.

"The controls are extremely delicate and complicated," Duncan went on. "You'd probably break something."

"Sorry," Nick muttered, embarrassed.

Duncan smiled apologetically.

"No," he said. "*I'm* sorry. Dr. Sakurai keeps telling me I need to work on my customer service skills, and I guess she's right. It's just that it takes a steady hand and a lot of experience to get Curiosity to do what you want it to. I'm only beginning to get the hang of it myself."

Nick glanced down at the control box again. Aside from a small view screen that showed what the robot's camera was pointed at—a Grow-Your-Own Fungus Farm Starter Kit at the moment—it didn't look any different from what you'd need to fly a model airplane. And any kid could do that with a little practice, right?

Still, Nick decided not to say so. Duncan was being sorta-kinda nice for once. Why contradict him?

And anyway, something else had caught Nick's eye.

It was on a low shelf behind the counter.

A row of robots.

There were nine of them, all about a foot tall. Eight were generic and clunky—like the angular, lumbering robots from goofy old movies, only with what looked like propellers stuck to their heads.

The ninth was different, though.

"Is that a robot *pirate*?" Nick asked.

Duncan turned, picked up the little figure Nick had noticed, and placed it on the counter.

It was wearing a buccaneer's plumed hat and oversized coat and broad, black belt. It even had a peg leg, though instead of being made of wood, it was metal.

Duncan waved a hand in front of its flat, silver face, and its eyes began to glow red.

"Arrrrrr," the robot said, waving a tiny cutlass it clutched in one of its hands. "Thank ye for setting sail for the Treasure Trove, me hearties!"

"Th-th-the Treasure Trove?" Nick spluttered.

Duncan was gazing admiringly at the robot pirate. He didn't seem to notice how surprised Nick was.

"Yeah. It's one of those antiques places up the street," he said. "Dr. Sakurai's been giving out toy robots all over town. As a promotional thing. She thinks people will notice them, ask where they came from, and then maybe come in here. That's what she and your uncle are doing right now, actually. They're over at the police station dropping off a robot cop."

"Ou-ou-our uncle?"

It was turning out to be a big day for spluttering.

"Yeah. Ol' Romeo," Duncan said. "He came in here with flowers that looked like they'd just been yanked out of somebody's yard."

Nick cringed. "They weren't begonias, were they?"

"I don't know. I'm not good with flowers."

"Sort of big and floppy and reddish pink?"

"Yeah. That was them. With roots and clumps of dirt still hanging off the bottom."

Nick sighed.

Their uncle's neighbor Julie had just planted a fresh bed of begonias.

If Uncle Newt wasn't careful, the day would come when Julie was planting *him* in her yard.

Tesla, Silas, and DeMarco appeared beside Nick, and Tesla plonked three small, plastic-coated packages on the counter.

Inside were three mini-vibration motors.

"Cool pirate," Tesla said to Duncan as he rang up the sale. "Did I hear him say something about the Treasure Trove?"

"Yeah. Dr. Sakurai offered it to the guy who owns the place, but he wouldn't take it. Said it would 'disrupt the store's old-fashioned, down-home charm.' Or something like that." Duncan looked at the total on the register. "That'll be ten dollars and forty-two cents."

Tesla produced a wad of crumpled bills.

"Nick," she said, "we need another dollar forty-two."

"I don't have a dollar forty-two. I don't have a penny."

Tesla shot her brother an irritated glare.

"Hey, when DeMarco got us this morning, it was for an emergency, not a shopping spree," Nick said. "How would I know we might need . . . excuse me. What are you doing?"

Duncan had pulled out his wallet and placed two ones on the little pile of bills on the countertop.

"Giving you that dollar forty-two," he said.

He gathered up the money, put it in the cash register, then gave himself the change.

"That was really nice. Thank you," said Tesla.

The boys all thanked Duncan, too.

He gave them an "it's nothing" shrug.

"It's good to see young people taking an interest in building things," he said. "It'll keep you out of trouble."

I wouldn't be so sure of that, Nick thought.

Tesla picked up the mini-vibration motors, thanked Duncan again, and led her brother and their friends out of the Wonder Hut.

It was decided that Nick and Tesla would go back to Uncle Newt's to build robo-bugs while Silas and Dc

Marco kept an eye on the Treasure Trove.

Actually, it wasn't so much decided as dictated.

"Why do you always get to tell everybody what to do?" DeMarco asked Tesla, who'd done the dictating.

"Because I'm the one who always knows what to do," Tesla said. "See you in a couple hours."

"A couple hours?" DeMarco moaned as Nick and Tesla headed off toward Hero Worship, Incorporated, where they'd left their bikes. "We can't just stand around for a couple hours. We went nuts with boredom before, and that was barely thirty minutes."

"Maybe we could get some more frozen yogurt," Silas suggested.

"We gave Tesla our last three bucks to help pay for those little whatchamacallits, remember?"

"Oh, yeah," Silas said. "We *will* go nuts."

Tesla didn't want to explain to Uncle Newt why they were in the basement building robotic bugs. Fortunately, she didn't have to.

When the kids got home, Uncle Newt wasn't there.

"He must still be out with Dr. Sakurai," Nick said.

"Duncan said he came by to bring her flowers this morning."

"I knew it," Tesla muttered with a roll of the eyes. "Newt and Hiroko, sittin' in a tree . . ."

Nick shivered. He didn't want to think about his uncle K-I-S-S-I-N-G.

He changed the subject by telling his sister about the robots Dr. Sakurai was giving out around town.

"What a cool lady," Tesla said. "I just can't believe she'd quit a job at the Jet Propulsion Laboratory to come here and sell train sets." She started down the stairs to the basement laboratory. "Anyway—come on. We've gotta get these things built before the Treasure Trove closes."

"Don't worry," Nick said. "I've already got a blueprint in my head."

"Me, too," said Tesla.

She just hoped their blueprints were the same.

They weren't.

"LED lights for eyes? Why?" Nick said. "That doesn't make any sense for a bug."

"So? Dobek has a bug phobia. An irrational fear. It doesn't *have* to make sense. We just need him to have a reaction."

"But the reaction can't be, 'How'd those weird little toys get in here?' It has to be, '*AHHHHHHH! Bugs!*'"

"Without the glowing eyes, he might not even notice the bug at all."

Nick looked skeptical.

"Of course, maybe the grape jelly would do the trick," Tesla said, thinking out loud.

"Grape jelly?" said Nick.

"Yeah. So the robot's dark and kind of shimmery like a roach and leaves a gooey mess behind when someone stomps on it. Maybe the glimmer of it would be enough to catch Dobek's attention."

"Don't you think a bunch of jelly's going to mess up our wiring?"

"We wouldn't need a *bunch*."

"One drop would be too much!"

"Maybe," Tesla said. "Maybe not."

"All right. Fine," Nick spat. "You can have the glowing eyes . . . *if* we lose the jelly."

"Done."

They shook on it.

"Now," Tesla said, "I was thinking we could make the bodies out of cardboard."

"What? Bottle caps would be a million times better."

"Bottle caps? Those wouldn't work at all."

"Would so!"

"Would not!"

They argued for a while until Tesla suggested they cut the heads of toothbrushes and use those. Nick thought that was brilliant.

Then they started arguing about the legs.

An hour later, Nick and Tesla had three glowing-eyed, toothbrush-bodied, wire-legged, jelly-free robo-bugs.

They also had twenty minutes to get them to the Treasure Trove before Dobek's mysterious buyer "Anton" showed up.

"Go, go, go!" Tesla said as she pushed her brother up the basement stairs.

"I'm going, I'm going, I'm going!" said Nick.

"Where, where, where?" said Uncle Newt.

He was dumping the contents of a can of Spaghettios into a huge pot on the stove top.

"Oh, nowhere," said Tesla. "Where have you been all day?"

Uncle Newt clutched his hands to his chest—apparently forgetting that one of them held an open can. Sludgy red tomato sauce spilled onto his white lab coat.

"Heaven," he said with a sigh.

Tesla groaned.

"We've really gotta go," said Nick.

"Enjoy nowhere!" Uncle Newt called after them as they bolted out the door. "But be back by five!"

It was already 4:44.

When Nick and Tesla had made their way downtown again, they found Silas and DeMarco still in their stakeout location outside It's-Froze-Yo!

DeMarco was trying to stand on Silas's shoulders.

"Stay still," DeMarco said as he wriggled and writhed on Silas's back, his hands wrapped around his friend's forehead.

“I *am* still,” Silas said.

DeMarco managed to get a foot up on one of Silas’s broad shoulders, but it quickly slid off again.

“I told you this would be easier if I knelt down first,” said Silas.

“But you’d never get up again once I was on your shoulders.”

“Yes, I would.”

“Uhhh . . . are you guys trying to get a better look into the Treasure Trove?” Nick asked.

“Nope,” said Silas.

“We were just bored,” said DeMarco.

DeMarco let go of Silas’s head and dropped to the ground.

“Well, thanks for staying inconspicuous,” Tesla said.

“You’re welcome,” Silas said with a smile.

DeMarco hadn’t missed the sarcasm, though.

“Hey, you guys were gone for, like, forever,” he said, “and there was nothing to see up there but people wandering around looking at junk.”

Nick and Tesla gazed up at the Treasure Trove. The lights were still on, but no one was in sight.

“Has Anton showed up?” Nick asked.

DeMarco shook his head. "We don't think so. No one's gone inside in, like, ten minutes."

"How much time do we have?" Silas asked.

"Not much," Nick told him. "Maybe five minutes."

Silas's eyes went wide. "What? Well, let's hurry up, then! If that Anthony guy gets his hands on the comic book before we do—"

"Anton," Nick corrected.

"We're not 'getting our hands on the comic book,' remember?" Tesla said. "We just want to be sure Dobek has it before we go to Sgt. Feiffer."

"Yeah, right, whatever." Silas looked down at the little doohickeys Nick was pulling from his jacket pocket. "Is that them? How'd they turn out?"

"See for yourself," Tesla said.

She leaned in close to her brother's cupped hands and connected the wires on the robo-bugs. The little robots began to vibrate, their eyes glowing red.

"Cool!" said Silas.

"They look fakey," said DeMarco.

"Fakey?" said Tesla.

"I told you the light-up eyes were too much," said Nick.

"*Fakey?*" Tesla said again.

DeMarco shrugged. "Sorry. They do. There's no way Dobek's going to be fooled by those things. Not for a second."

"Well, I think he's gonna freak," said Silas.

DeMarco shook his head. "He's not gonna freak."

"He *is* gonna freak," said Silas.

"He's *not* gonna freak," said DeMarco.

"He *is* gonna freak."

"He's *not* gonna freak."

"He *is* gonna freak."

"He's *not* gonna—"

"Hey!" Tesla barked. "There's only one way to find out, right?"

"Right!" said Silas.

He snatched the robo-bugs out of Nick's hand and took off running.

"What are you doing?" a stunned Nick yelled after him.

Silas was already halfway across the street.

Car tires screeched. A horn honked. But Silas just kept going.

"Come back!" Tesla called out. "We need to discuss the plan!"

Silas reached the steps to the Treasure Trove and

started bounding up two at a time.

"Hide!" DeMarco cried. He grabbed Nick and Tesla and dragged them along with him as he ducked behind a nearby trash can. "Dobek's looking!"

The three kids crouched down and hid. After a few seconds, they risked a look up at the Treasure Trove, DeMarco peeking around one side of the garbage can, Nick around the other, and Tesla peering over the top.

Dobek was still standing at one of his store's open windows, looking down at the street. He didn't seem to notice them. Eventually, he turned away and disappeared.

"Now what?" Nick said.

Tesla stood up. "Now we just have to hope that—"

"*EEEEEEEEEEEEEEEEEEEEEEEEEEEEEEE!*"

The kids looked up at the Treasure Trove again.

Dobek was running past the windows waving his hands in the air.

"Ugh! No! Horrible! Nasty! Legs! Eyes! Scurrying! Dirty!" he shrieked. "*EEEEEEEEEEEEEEEEEEEEEEEEEEE!*"

"Well, how about that?" DeMarco said. "He freaked."

Silas rushed out of the Treasure Trove and started hurrying down the steps to the sidewalk at a pace just shy of a scramble. There was something flat and rectangular and yellowish clutched in his hands.

A manila envelope.

When he reached the bottom of the stairs, Silas turned right and rushed up the street. No one seemed to notice him as he barreled past and disappeared around the corner. Everyone was looking up at the Treasure Trove.

"AAAAAAAAAAAAAAAAAAAA! Icky icky evil! Die die DIE!"

“Come on,” Tesla said.

She hurried away, Nick and DeMarco behind her. They turned at the first corner and headed down the street Silas had used for his getaway. It was a lot darker and dirtier than Main Street—the only businesses on the block were a hole-in-the-wall convenience store and a grungy little laundromat—and Silas was nowhere to be seen.

“Where’d he go?” Nick said.

“I don’t know,” said Tesla. “He’s gotta be around here somewhere. He’s not that faAAAAAAAA!”

A large, shadowy shape was lunging at her from a nearby alley.

“Now I’ve got you meddling kids!” it cried.

Tesla and Nick and DeMarco screamed.

The large, shadowy shape—Silas—laughed and laughed.

Tesla folded her arms across her chest and scowled at him. “And to think just a couple hours ago I called you a genius.”

“And you were right,” Silas said, beaming.

He held up the manila envelope he’d taken from the Treasure Trove.

“*Keep that out of sight*,” Tesla snapped, shooing

Silas back into the alley. "You weren't supposed to take it. You were just supposed to make sure the comic book was really there."

Silas's smile faded as his friends followed him into the alley, looking like they wanted to throw him into the nearest Dumpster.

"I wasn't going to just leave it for Antonio," he protested.

"Anton," Nick said.

Silas ignored him. "I had a chance to get it, so I got it."

"Did Dobek see you?" Tesla asked.

Silas shook his head, his grin returning. "Nah. The envelope was right under the cash register, like you and Nick guessed, and Dobek was too busy screaming about devil roaches to notice me running in and grabbing it." He waggled his eyebrows at DeMarco. "Told ya he'd freak."

"I know, I know," said DeMarco.

"So you've seen the comic?" Tesla asked. "It's okay?"

"Oh. Well. No," Silas said. "I haven't checked it yet. Guess I'd better, huh? It still needs to be in mint condition to bring in the big bucks. I swear, if Dobek so much as left a thumbprint on the cover, I'm going back there with a whole *swarm* of robot bugs."

After a quick glance up and down the alley, Silas opened the envelope—the top flap was unsealed—and slowly, carefully slid out its contents.

"Ta-da!" he started to say.

It came out "Ta-*chuh*?"

The kids were looking down at a black-and-white picture of a small, smiling man leaning against R2-D2, the famous movie droid. Written in cursive in the top left corner were the words, "Hello! Bleep bloop! Kenny Baker."

"Who's Kenny Baker?" said Tesla.

DeMarco pointed at the picture. "He's the actor inside R2-D2. Duh."

"There's an actor in R2-D2?" said Nick. "He's not a real robot?"

DeMarco fixed him with an "are you kidding or crazy?" stare.

"Uhhh, no. R2-D2 is not really a robot."

Nick wilted.

"I feel so betrayed."

Silas tilted the envelope and gave it a shake, but nothing else came out.

"Oh, noooooooo," Silas moaned.

"I can't believe it," Tesla said. "You grabbed the wrong package."

"But, but, but . . . look!"

Silas flipped the envelope over and pointed to two words written on the other side.

ANTON BISCHOFF

"See?" Silas said. "It's for Antoine!"

Nick didn't bother correcting him this time. Instead, he turned to his sister.

"You know, we never did hear Dobek say anything about a comic book, Tez. He just mentioned having something Anton wanted. Maybe the guy collects *Star Wars* stuff."

Tesla slapped a hand across her forehead. "Which would mean we were wrong about Dobek. We set out to catch a thief . . . and now we're thieves ourselves."

Nick nodded. "It sure looks that way."

"Not," she said, "good."

"Yeah. But it could be worse," DeMarco said. "At least we didn't get cau—"

"Nick, Tesla!" a man yelled. "And . . . umm . . . the

other two!"

The kids spun around to find Sgt. Feiffer of the Half Moon Bay Police Department blocking the entrance to the alley with his little three-wheeled "squad car." (Budget cuts had forced the town to sell off all its police vehicles except for a single meter reader's cart.)

"What are you up to back there?" Sgt. Feiffer shouted, peering at them from the driver's seat (which was actually the only seat the cart had).

Silas quickly slipped the envelope behind his back.

Nick, Tesla, and DeMarco all spoke at once.

"We're looking for rats," said Nick.

"We're looking for loose change," said Tesla.

"We're trying to find the sunglasses I borrowed from my dad and then lost when I was skateboarding this afternoon, and he's going to kill me if I can't find them but I'm pretty sure they're around here someplace," said DeMarco.

Sgt. Feiffer looked confused.

He was a small, mild-mannered man with balding gray hair and a fondness for short-sleeved work shirts and wide, striped ties. If Nick hadn't known he was Half Moon Bay's one-man police force, he would've assumed he was an insurance salesman or an accountant or maybe a substitute teacher.

"Uhh . . . I guess we're kind of killing three birds with one stone," Tesla said. "You know. As long as we're looking for the sunglasses."

"Got it," Sgt. Feiffer said. "Why rats, though?"

"Well . . . umm . . . you know . . ."

"Rats are cool!" DeMarco blurted out.

"Yeah, yeah! Cool!" said Nick.

"So cool," said Tesla.

"The coolest," said Silas.

Sgt. Feiffer gaped at them a moment, then shook his head and chuckled.

"If you say so," he said, adding a muttered "kids today."

"So," Tesla said, "how's the big investigation going?"

Sgt. Feiffer threw Silas a quizzical look.

"What?" Silas said, startled. Then he realized what the look meant. "Oh. I told them all about the robbery."

He still had his hands behind his back, and sweat had begun beading on his face as he shifted his weight nervously from foot to foot.

"Well," Sgt. Feiffer said, turning back to Tesla, "to be honest, I don't have much to work with. I spoke to April Barnett—the woman who sold Mr. Kuskie the comic book at the estate sale—and I believe her when she says she had no idea it was valuable. When I told her what it was worth, she nearly fainted. I also spoke to the only other person of interest in the case. I don't want to name names, but—"

"You're talking about Mr. Dobek," Tesla said.

Sgt. Feiffer chuckled.

"Boy. Not a big one for keeping secrets, are you?" he said to Silas.

Silas just smiled weakly and wiped the sweat out

of his eyes with his free hand.

"Does Mr. Dobek have an alibi for last night?" Tesla asked.

"If he didn't, I wouldn't tell you. But he does, so I will," Sgt. Feiffer said. "Yes. He has an alibi. He went up to Sonoma County last night for a concert. The Summer Reggae Regatta at the Mountain Pass Winery. Spent the night at a La Quinta Inn—for which he has a receipt—and got a speeding ticket rushing back down here in the morning to open his store. I've confirmed that with the Highway Patrol. Alibis don't get much more rock solid than that. It's funny, though . . ."

"What?" Nick said.

"Yeah. What is it, Sergeant?" said Tesla.

They both leaned forward slightly, eager to hear the brilliant deduction that would blow Dobek's "rock solid alibi" apart.

"I never would have pegged Dobek for a reggae fan," Sgt. Feiffer said. "Seems more like a classical music kind of guy."

Nick and Tesla slumped.

"So . . . now you don't have any suspects at all," Tesla said.

“That’s about the size of it. Hey . . . maybe I should get you kids to help me with the case. You’re a bunch of ace detectives, am I right?” Sgt. Feiffer laughed.

“Ha,” said Tesla.

“Ha ha,” said Nick.

“Ha ha ha,” said DeMarco.

Silas wiped more sweat from his face.

“Anyhoo,” Sgt. Feiffer said, turning to DeMarco, “I’ve got a free minute. Want me to help you find those sunglasses?”

“Sunglasses?” Silas said. “What sunglasses?”

“My dad’s sunglasses . . . remember?” DeMarco said.

He elbowed his friend so hard Silas lost his grip on the envelope.

Half a second before it hit the sidewalk, Sgt. Feiffer’s cell phone began blasting “Jailhouse Rock.”

“Excuse me. I have to take this,” Sgt. Feiffer said. He turned his back to the kids and put the phone to his ear. “Feiffer here. Go.”

Silas took the opportunity to whip around and pick up the envelope.

DeMarco took the opportunity to punch Silas on the arm.

"Another one?" Sgt. Feiffer said into his phone, oblivious to what was going on behind him. "Unbelievable. Looks like we've got a crime wave on our hands. All right, I'm right around the corner from the Treasure Trove. Tell him I'll be right there."

He hung up and turned around just in time to see Silas punching DeMarco back.

"No need to fight over a quarter, guys," Tesla said. "We're splitting everything we find four ways, remember?"

"Oh," DeMarco said. "Right."

"What?" said Silas.

DeMarco looked like he wanted to punch him again.

Tesla looked like she wanted to join in.

"Sorry, kids," said Sgt. Feiffer. "Duty calls. There's been another theft."

"My goodness," said Tesla.

"How shocking," said Nick.

"What is the world coming to?" said DeMarco.

Silas was finally learning to keep his big mouth shut.

"Good luck with the sunglasses," Sgt. Feiffer said. "And don't stay out too late looking for 'em. Half

Moon Bay has a ten o'clock curfew for minors, you know. I'd hate to have to throw you kids in the clink!"

Nick, Tesla, and DeMarco all *ha ha ha*-ed.

Silas kept playing it safe and stayed silent.

Sgt. Feiffer finally put his cart in gear and drove off at top speed—about six miles an hour.

"Great," Nick groaned. "Now he's going to be after us instead of whoever stole the comic book."

"So what do we do?" asked DeMarco.

"That's obvious," said Tesla. "We have to return the R2-D2 autograph to Dobek."

"But we'll get in trouble!" said Nick.

"Big trouble!" said DeMarco.

"*Huge* trouble!" said Silas. "And then we'll never get the comic book back and my dad will lose his store and I'll end up freezing to death in a ditch because we'll have sold all our clothes to buy old bologna and moldy bread at the grocery outlet after we've run out of—"

"Silas! Geez! We can't get caught returning the photo! I get it!" Tesla broke in. "That's why we're going to be—"

Tesla caught herself, took a deep breath, and dropped her voice to a whisper.

"That's why we're going to be sneaky."

The boys agreed. Sneaky—that was the way to get the photograph back into the Treasure Trove.

Sneaky how, though? That was what none of them knew. And they didn't have time to figure it out.

If Silas and DeMarco were late for dinner, they might get in trouble. Maybe not big, *huge* trouble, but big enough. How can you break into an antiques store when you're grounded?

So it was agreed that the four of them would meet up after dark to plan their next move. Tesla insisted on keeping the autographed picture in the meantime. She wanted to test ways to get it into the store, she said. Which was probably *mostly* true. Nick had a hunch there was another reason, too.

Not only was Silas the world's worst secret-keeper, he was also forgetful. Let him hang onto the picture, and he'd either end up showing it to his dad or leaving it by the Slurpee machine at the 7-Eleven.

So when Nick and Tesla came pedaling up to Uncle Newt's house, the photo was tucked away in the place Tesla had decided would be the safest and most discreet: under Nick's shirt.

Nick was glad the ride home was almost over.

Manila envelopes really chafe.

"Hey," Nick said as he and Tesla swooped up the driveway, "who does that belong to?"

A red car was parked behind the Newtmobile.

"I don't know," Tesla said, "but I like the name."

It was a model of electric car they'd read about before: the Tesla.

"What if it's Dobek?" Nick said as he and Tesla walked their bikes into the garage. "Or Anton What's-His-Name?"

"How would they know to come here?" Tesla asked.

"Maybe Silas told someone."

"Oh, come on. We haven't seen Silas in, what, eight minutes? Even he can keep his mouth shut that long."

Nick gave his sister a dubious look.

"Right," she said. "Hide the envelope behind the cat food."

When Nick and Tesla went inside, they found their uncle hanging next to the dining room table. This was nothing new: Uncle Newt preferred to eat "astronaut style" and had bolted straps to the ceiling so he could buckle himself in and simulate weightlessness.

What *was* new was that he wasn't alone.

Hiroko Sakurai was hanging beside him.

"Hi, guys!" she said with a smile.

"Grab a bowl and help yourself to some Spaghettios!" said Uncle Newt. "I put out carrot sticks and bagels, too!"

That made it one of the fanciest meals Uncle Newt had ever prepared.

"Oh, boy," Nick said with a feeble smile. "Bagels."

But he didn't end up taking any, even though Uncle Newt had built a pyramid of them in the kitchen nearly a foot high.

Eureka the cat was up on the counter methodically licking bagel after bagel, his bald butt surrounded by soggy-looking crumbs.

Nick and Tesla sighed and served themselves Spaghettios and carrots.

On the counter beside the carrots and bagels and cat butt were the Teslanator and Frank the robot.

"We were just admiring your creations," Dr. Sakurai said as Nick and Tesla seated themselves at the dining room table.

"My robot looked a lot better before a bike ran over it," Tesla said.

"I'm sure it did," said Dr. Sakurai. "Still, the motor wasn't totally crushed. I could see the modifications you'd made with tape so it would vibrate. That was really clever. I used to build my own robots when I was your age, but they were mostly rubber bands and shoe boxes. Not nearly as sophisticated as yours."

Tesla brightened. "Thanks."

She took a bite of Spaghettios, and her expression soured again. She'd forgotten how much she disliked Spaghettios.

"If it was your lifelong dream to build robots, why

did you quit the Jet Propulsion Lab and move back here?" Nick asked.

He shoveled a spoonful of Spaghettios into his mouth. He usually didn't mind them at all, especially the kind with the little meatballs.

"I guess I got tired of building robots for other people. And with other people," Dr. Sakurai said. "Every one of my ideas had to be approved by a team, a supervisor, a manager, a director. By the time the idea got to the very top, it would be distorted beyond all recognition, and the answer was usually 'no.' So many middlemen. So many rules. It was stifling."

As she spoke, Dr. Sakurai's face hardened, her tone turned bitter.

Then she caught herself and smiled again.

"Fortunately," she said, "I heard all kinds of stories about a brilliant scientist who left JPL and started making amazing breakthroughs in his own basement. I found that inspiring."

Dr. Sakurai looked over at Uncle Newt.

He was blushing so much, it looked like he'd smeared Spaghettios sauce across his face. But he managed to meet Dr. Sakurai's gaze, and for a long, silent moment the two of them just looked into each other's eyes.

A song echoed inside Nick's head.

Newt and Hiroko, sittin' in a tree . . .

He suddenly found that he'd lost his appetite for Spaghettios, too.

Tesla grew so uncomfortable she scooched her chair back from the table and asked if anyone wanted another bagel.

"No, thank you," Dr. Sakurai said. "I should probably be getting back to the Wonder Hut. Duncan would keep working all night if I let him—he'd never leave!—but I prefer to close up myself."

She began unbuckling herself with surprising deftness, considering that (one had to assume) she'd never been strung up like a piñata before.

"Duncan's a lot nicer now that you own the store," Nick said. "Not that he was ever mean. But he used to just kind of ignore us."

Dr. Sakurai swung down gracefully and planted her feet on the floor.

"Duncan has worked in that store so long, I think his best friends are model trains and airplanes," she said. "I've been encouraging him to take an interest in people."

"You seem to be good at that," Tesla said with a meaningful look at her uncle.

He didn't notice. He just kept gazing worshipfully at Dr. Sakurai.

"Well, good night," Dr. Sakurai said. "I hope I'll see you again soon."

"Oh, you will! You will!" Uncle Newt said. "But don't go yet! Let me walk you to your car!"

He was in such a hurry to unstrap himself he plummeted straight down and crashed face-first into the floor.

Once Dr. Sakurai was sure he hadn't broken his nose, she let him escort her outside.

"I know Uncle Newt's our family," Tesla said. "And that he's taking care of us."

"Sort of," grumbled Nick, forlornly stirring his Spaghettios. They were room temperature now, and the sauce had started to congeal.

"But I don't get what Dr. Sakurai sees in him," Tesla went on.

"Brains," said Nick.

"Yeah. But look what they're wrapped in."

The phone in the kitchen rang, and Nick hopped from his seat and ran to answer it.

“It only shows the number. No name,” he said when he checked the caller I.D. “And I don’t recognize the area code!”

He didn’t say “Maybe it’s Uzbekistan,” but the excitement in his voice did.

“Hello? Oh.”

Nick hung up and slunk back to the table.

“It was a recording,” he said. “Apparently, there’s never been a better time to refinance our mortgage.”

“Now that’s what *real* evil robots are like,” Tesla said. “They’re not trying to take over the world. They just make annoying phone calls at dinnertime.”

Tesla took a loud bite from her biggest carrot stick, then picked up her bowl and headed for the kitchen.

“Come on,” she said. “We’ve got work to do.”

Nick turned in a circle, taking in every bit of bric-a-brac in their uncle’s cluttered basement lab.

He and Tesla had been down there for half an hour, and they still hadn’t figured out a sneaky way to return the photograph Silas had stolen

Nick pointed at a plasma emission spectrometer. "Maybe we could—"

"Already thought of it," Tesla said, shaking her head. "Won't work."

Nick pointed at a chassis dynamometer. "Maybe we could—"

"Already thought of it. Won't work."

Nick pointed at a tuba. "Maybe we could—"

"Already thought of it. Won't work."

"Fine! *You* come up something!"

"All right. I will."

Tesla turned in a circle.

She ended up pointing at a sledgehammer.

"Maybe we could—"

"Already thought of it," Nick said. "Won't work."

A little while later, Uncle Newt came downstairs to tinker with the newest model of his compost-powered vacuum cleaner. He couldn't seem to stay focused, though. After just a couple minutes' work, he started picking rotten black banana nubs out of the compost chamber and flicking them at the wall.

“She loves me,” he said. “She loves me not. She loves me. She loves me not.”

The slimy nubs stuck to the wall with a sickening little *splitch splitch splitch.*

“Come on,” Tesla said to Nick. “It’s almost time for that PBS special about genome mapping.”

“Oooo! Right!”

Uncle Newt didn’t even seem to notice Nick and Tesla as they headed for the stairs.

“She love me,” he said dreamily. “She loves me not.”

Splitch splitch splitch . . .

Not long after Nick and Tesla went upstairs, there was a gentle knock on the back door. It was pitch black outside, but they knew who it was.

Nick opened the door, and Silas and DeMarco came in.

“Where’s your uncle?” DeMarco asked.

“The usual,” Tesla said.

She nodded at the door to the basement.

DeMarco eyed it nervously, as he always did. He

may have been a daredevil at heart, but even a daredevil can get a little edgy around a door covered with signs reading HAZARDOUS, FLAMMABLE, POISON, HIGH VOLTAGE, DANGER.

"Did you figure out how we're gonna get the thingamajig back to Dobek without giving away who took it?" he said.

Nick and Tesla shook their heads glumly.

"That's okay!" Silas said cheerfully. "I've got a plan!"

He handed Tesla a piece of paper.

Nick leaned over to review it with her.

YUM!
THE TREASURE TROVE
ENVELOPE
OPEN WINDOW
DEAD SQUIRREL
ME
GO SILAS!

"Only we shouldn't really use an eagle," Silas said. "It'd be a lot easier to catch a pigeon. And that way we could just throw, like, an old sandwich instead of roadkill."

"Uhh," said Nick, "so the envelope is tied to the bird's beak . . . ?"

Silas nodded excitedly.

"And it flies into the store after the food?"

Silas nodded again.

"And when the bird opens its mouth to eat the food . . ."

"The string comes loose, the envelope drops to the floor, and we go find the *real* comic book thief!" Silas declared.

Nick kept squinting skeptically at the drawing. "How can the eagle say 'yum' with its beak tied shut?"

"Oh," Silas said. "I guess he's just mumbling it."

"And why do we look like midgets?"

Silas shrugged. "That's just how you look to me."

"I don't think you're asking the right questions," DeMarco said to Nick.

Nick sighed.

The only "right question" he could think of was

"Silas, are you nuts?" But he didn't think he should ask it.

Instead, he turned to his sister, about to say "Back to the drawing board."

To his surprise, though, she looked thrilled, not bewildered.

"Silas," she said, "you're a genius again!"

Silas beamed. "I am?"

"He is?" said Nick and DeMarco.

"Yes," Tesla said firmly. "He is."

And she stretched out a finger and tapped two words on Silas's blueprint:

OPEN WINDOW

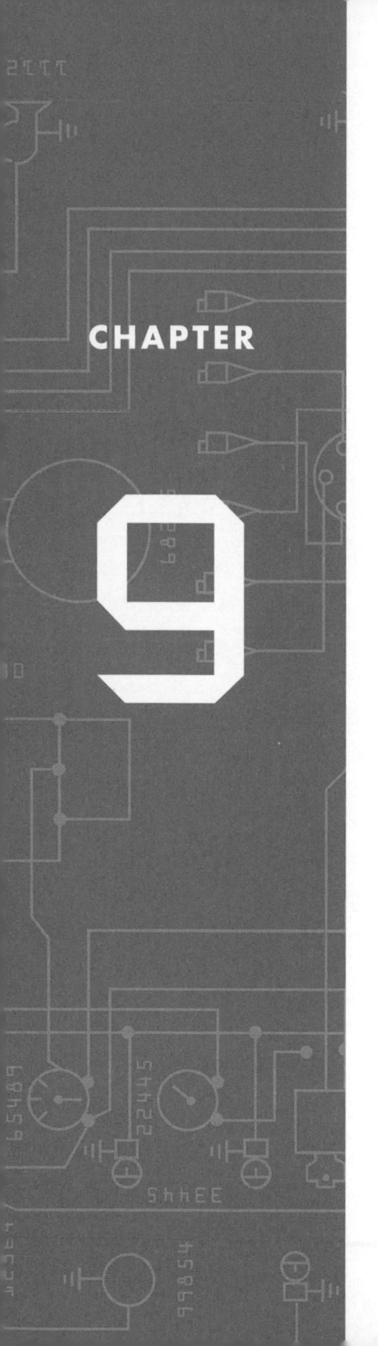

"Really?" Nick said when his sister sketched out her idea.

Tesla nodded. "Really."

"Come on," said DeMarco. "Really?"

Tesla nodded even harder. "Yes. Really."

"But . . . *really* really?" said Nick.

"Yes! *Really* really! I think it would work! Geez!"

"I don't know why you guys aren't into it," Silas said to Nick and DeMarco. He turned to grin at Tesla. "It sounds like a great idea to me."

Tesla started having second thoughts.

A few hours later, Nick and Tesla were on Main Street looking up at the Treasure Trove.

One of the windows was open, just as it had been that afternoon.

It was midnight, and no one else was around—not even Silas and DeMarco.

DeMarco had to be home by eight thirty, Silas by nine. Nick and Tesla, on the other hand, never had any set bedtime.

"Just turn off the lights when you get tired," Uncle Newt would say. "I'll be down in the lab."

Tesla's plan didn't require four people anyway. Two could get the job done while having a better chance of getting away unseen. In fact, one person would probably be best of all, but neither Nick nor Tesla would let the other go alone.

So there they both were on a dark, deserted street pulling what looked like a basketball made out of bread from Tesla's backpack.

At the center of the big ball—which was actually a dozen slightly cat-chewed bagels stuck together with glue—was the envelope Silas had taken from the Treasure Trove.

A photograph would be too light and not aerodynamic enough to throw through a second-story window. But give it some weight and the right shape, and it should be as easy as shooting a free throw . . . or so Tesla thought.

"You keep lookout," Nick said, looking up at the open window. "I'll throw the bagels."

"Why you?"

"I'm better at basketball than you are."

"True."

Tesla turned toward Main Street, her gaze sweeping from north to south to north to south.

Even if they weren't caught with the stolen picture, they could get in trouble. They were breaking Half Moon Bay's curfew for kids, for one thing. And they'd never been out so late before without an adult along. Who knew what went on after midnight, even in a quiet little town like Half Moon Bay? It was creepy to think about—so Tesla did her best not to think.

Of course, *not* thinking wasn't her style.

"Hurry up," she said. "I want to get out of here."

"Like I want to stay here all night?" Nick snapped

ART GALLERY
WINE SHOP
HALF

back. "I'm going as fast as I can."

He'd been taking careful aim, and now he brought the bagelball up and made his shot.

The bagels hit the side of the building and dropped back down to the sidewalk.

"Oh, come *on*," Tesla groaned.

"That window's up a lot higher than a basketball hoop," Nick said. "I've got the range now, though."

He scooped up the bagels, gave the open window a long look, and tried again.

The bagels thumped into the glass, fell, and bounced off the back of Tesla's head.

"*Nnnnnnnick*," Tesla growled.

"I'll get it next time for sure! I promise!"

Nick picked up the bagels again. Some were crumbling. Others were coming loose.

One more smack against the glass, and the whole thing might fly apart.

Nick brought up the bagelball, whispered "this time . . . please," and lobbed it heavenward.

The bagels soared in a graceful arc up to and through the open window.

"Swish!" said Nick.

"Car!" said Tesla.

Headlights came sweeping along the street.

Nick and Tesla scrambled to the stairs leading to the Treasure Trove, leapt up a few steps, and pressed themselves against the side of the building.

"Oh, no!" Nick said. "The backpack!"

It had been abandoned on the sidewalk in plain view.

"We just have to hope it's not noticed," Tesla said.

A white pickup truck cruised up the street toward them. It didn't seem to slow down at all as it passed Nick and Tesla and the backpack. It just kept moving smoothly up Main Street until it was gone.

Nick blew out a breath. "Man, that was close. I thought for a second we were—"

There was a distant *pop* like the sound of a cherry bomb exploding, then the clitter-clatter of breaking glass.

"What was that?" Nick asked.

A wide-eyed Tesla put a hand on her brother's head and turned it ten degrees to the left.

Nick found himself looking across the street at the business next to It's-Froze-Yo! Painted on the display window were the words JEWELRY BY ANGELA. The "Angela" had a halo over the "A" and little wings sprouting from the "L."

A beam of light was moving around on the other side of the glass, cutting through swirls of sooty smoke inside the store.

"Maybe it's just the owner or a security guy checking the place," Nick said.

"After setting it on fire?"

The light bounced off something made of glass at the back of the store, then winked out as a figure draped in black moved in front of the reflection.

"*Dressed as a ninja?*" said Tesla.

"Oh, man!" said Nick. "It's a robbery! What do we do?"

"We go in for a closer look."

Nick was about to say "You're joking, right?" But Tesla answered his question before he could even ask it.

She started going in for a closer look.

"Tez, no!" Nick called from the shadows. "You're supposed to run away from dangerous criminals, not go toward them."

"What if it's the thief who stole Mr. Kuskie's comic?" Tesla said without glancing back. "We could wrap up the mystery right now."

“Or we could get ourselves killed right now. Tesla, stop!”

She didn’t seem to be listening, though. She just kept walking toward the jewelry store—and the jewelry *thief*—on the other side of the street.

The flashlight beam, meanwhile, had begun moving again, toward the center of the store. When it stopped, it seemed to be pointed downward. Then it swung up so that it was shining directly into the display window at the front of the store.

It froze there for a moment—long enough for Nick to realize that the thief was looking out through the window at the street.

And at Tesla.

“He sees you, Tez! We’ve gotta get out of here!”

The light whipped away from the window, moved to the left, and settled for a few seconds on something on the wall. Then it began dancing spastically across the ceiling, growing smaller and fainter.

The thief was running away.

Tesla broke into a sprint toward the store.

A blaring blast stopped her after six steps.

CLANGA-LANGA-LANGA-LANGA-LANGA-LANGA.

An alarm was going off in the jewelry store.

“*Now* the alarm goes off?” Nick said. “When the guy’s leaving? Well, that’s just great!”

Tesla spun around and charged back toward her brother. By the time she made it to the sidewalk, another set of headlights was moving toward them up Main Street.

“Go, go, go, go, go!” Tesla yelled, snatching up the backpack.

It seemed really unnecessary to Nick—he was going!—but he didn’t stop to say so.

He and Tesla dashed around the corner to the alley where they’d stashed their bikes, and soon they were racing away into the night.

Tesla started to slow down once they were in Uncle Newt’s neighborhood on the other side of the highway, but Nick circled back and told her to hurry up.

“Why?” she said. “We got away from the scene of the crime.”

“Yeah . . . and so did that burglar, remember? For all we know, he’s out looking for us right now.”

“Oh. Good point.”

Tesla pedaled hard all the way home.

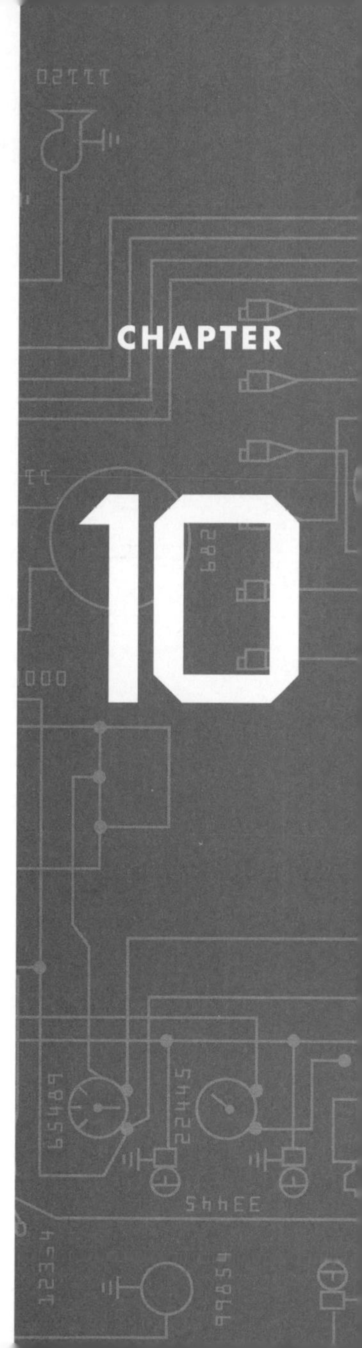

CHAPTER 10

"Whew," Tesla sighed as she closed the back door to Uncle Newt's house.

"What do you mean 'whew'?" Nick said. "You 'whew' too easily, do you know that? Whoever was in that jewelry store saw you for sure and might have seen me, and this isn't a big town so we might have been recognized, and if we were it wouldn't be hard to find us, so it might just be a matter of time before—"

"All right, all right! I get it!"

Tesla turned around and locked the door.

"Now can I 'whew'?" she said.

"What? No way! Anyone who

can break into a jewelry store isn't going to be stopped by that little lock."

"Let me guess," Tesla sighed. "You think we should hook the intruder alert system back up."

"Yes. I do."

"Even though it's almost one in the morning."

"Yes. Even though it's almost one in the morning."

"And even though I'm about to strangle you."

"Yes. Even though you're about to strangle me. Better you than that burglar."

"Fine."

Tesla headed toward the stairs.

Scattered around their room on the second floor were many of the gadgets and improvised devices they'd constructed that summer, including the Intruder Alert System—a simple circuit they'd made using quarters, wire, paper, batteries, and a bulb from a string of Christmas lights. If anyone tried to sneak into the house, the light in their room would turn on to warn them.

"You just can't let me relax, can you?" Tesla grumbled as she stomped up the hall.

"Maybe you should have thought of that before you got us mixed up in this mess."

“Oh, come on. I’m just trying to help a—where are you going?” Tesla said.

Nick had been following her, but now he was doubling back toward the kitchen.

“Forgot to do something,” he said.

He went around a corner and disappeared from view. But Tesla knew what he was doing: completing his nightly pre-bedtime ritual.

Tesla heard him pick up the phone, punch in some numbers, then hang up again. It was all over in less than ten seconds. Which meant the usual.

No message from their parents.

Nick came back from the kitchen looking gloomy—which was also the usual.

“Do you ever get the feeling we’re never gonna hear from Mom and Dad again?” he said.

“No,” Tesla said firmly. “I don’t.”

It was a lie. But it was the one she knew her brother needed to hear.

“Now come on,” Tesla said as she headed up the stairs. “That intruder alert system isn’t going to wire itself, and if I’m not in bed by two I *am* going to strangle you.”

They were in bed by one thirty, but the intruder alert system didn't help Tesla sleep any more soundly. Instead, she kept waking every ten minutes to either sit up and check the light or tell her brother to *stop* doing the exact same thing. Neither she nor Nick fell deeply asleep until birds were chirping outside and gray sunlight was beginning to seep in around the blinds.

When they finally woke up again and stumbled downstairs for breakfast, Uncle Newt was already hanging next to the dining room table eating a late *lunch*.

"Well, look who's slinking out of their cave," he said, looking up from his bowl of leftover Spaghettios. "It's practically July, you know. You're only supposed to hibernate in the winter."

"Says the man with a Christmas tree in his hallway," Tesla muttered.

She was always a little grouchy until she'd had her first Pop-Tart.

"Touché," Uncle Newt said with a good-natured grin.

He took a copy of the local newspaper off the table and disappeared behind it.

Nick and Tesla shuffled into the kitchen to get their breakfast.

Nick made it back to the table first. (His preferred breakfast was Cocoa Puffs and Cap'n Crunch mixed together in the same bowl, so he didn't have to wait for anything to toast.) When Tesla joined him with her Pop-Tart a moment later, he elbowed her in the ribs before she could take her first bite.

"What?" she snapped at him.

He jerked his chin at their uncle.

"Che eh oo," he said.

Translation: *Check it out.*

(Tesla had gotten pretty good at understanding her brother when he talked with his mouth full.)

Tesla looked at Uncle Newt. All she saw of him were his fingers wrapped around the edges of the *Half Moon Bay Guardian-Defender*.

Despite its impressive name, the *Guardian-Defender* was just a thin collection of city council minutes and coupons that showed up every afternoon whether you wanted it to or not. The kids tended to ignore it. The biggest news story was usually something like

"Area Woman Turns 96" or "Libarry Hosts Gala Lasagnae Fundriser." (There were always *lots* of misspelled words.)

There was an especially large headline on this day's front page.

Downtown Jeweler Hit by Rubbery

For a few confused seconds, Tesla wondered, "Hit by a rubbery *what?*"

Then it dawned on her.

Hit by *robbery*.

She squinted at the article, but the newsprint was too small for her to read from across the table.

"Oh, boy! That's so wonderful!" she squealed, clapping her hands. "They did it!"

"Huh?" said Uncle Newt, peering around the paper.

"Chuh?" said Nick through another mouthful of cereal.

Tesla pointed at the front page of the *Guardian-Defender*.

"Silas and DeMarco's friends!" Tesla said. "The swimmers!"

“Vuh schwimmuhs?” Nick said.

Uncle Newt looked at the front page.

The headline just to the left of “Downtown Jeweler Hit by Rubbery” was “Local Teens Snag Hunorable Mention at Synchronized Swimming Comtepetion.”

“You know these kids?” Uncle Newt asked.

Tesla nodded. “Sure. They don’t live too far from here.”

Uncle Newt looked at Nick.

He finally swallowed his cereal.

“Oh, yeah. Great couple kids,” he said. “So dedicated to their sport. We see them out in their pool . . . uhh . . . synchronizing every day. They’re really, really . . . synchronous.”

“Can we read the article about them?” Tesla asked her uncle.

“Sure,” he said. “Once I’ve finished the—”

Tesla leaned across the table and snatched the paper from his hands.

“Thanks, Uncle Newt!”

She spread out the *Guardian-Defender* and started reading, Nick peeking around her shoulder.

Of course, they weren’t reading about synchronized swimmers.

Downtown Half Moon Bay was the sceene of a daring heist last night when thieves struck Main Street's Jewelry by Angela (see ad, page 8). According to the store's owner, Angela Allbritten, the culprit used an explosive to get through the back door, then opened the supposedly burglar-proof safe in which she stores her most valuable stock. Though an alarm was triped, the culprit was gone by the time police responded to a call from Allbritten's security service.

"I give those jokers at Depend-Alarm $300 a month, and this is what I get?" a visibly upset Allbitten tlod the *Guardian-Defender*. "And that safe? How can they even call it a safe? It's not safe! They should call it an unsafe! I'm going to sue those clones, I swear it."

"Clones?" said Nick.

"I think it's supposed to be 'clowns,'" said Tesla.

Uncle Newt looked up from his Spaghettios. “Clones? Clowns? I thought you guys were reading about synchronized swimming.”

“Oh, we are,” Tesla said. “Gertrude and Herbert’s routine has a circus theme.”

“Gertrude and Herbert?”

“You know. The kids.” Tesla jabbed at a random spot on the front page. “Ooooh! They got an 8.8 from the judges!”

“Woo-hoo!” Nick cheered. “That’s better than they did with their synchronized salute to the four food groups!”

Uncle Newt shrugged and went back to eating.

Nick and Tesla went back to reading.

> Allbritten lost more than $2,5000 worth of merchandise, including a valuable new assortment of dimond engagement rings that had just arrived that afternoon. A custom-made robotic angel—a gift from the fine folks at Half Moon Bay hobby emporium the Wonder Hut (see ad, page 11)—was taken as well. Yet despite all

> that, the stroe's spunky owner vows to keep offering the area's finest selection of mid-range jewelry, jems, and precious stones at rock-bottom prices.
>
> "The real steals are the ones our customers get every day," Allbritten said. "Our prices are so low, they ouhgt to be a crime!"
>
> Law enforcement sources say they're searching for either one or more suspects, perhaps male or perhaps female, of indeterminate race, between the ages of 9 and 90.
>
> Bring this article in to Jewelry by Angela for 10% off yur first purchase of $200 or more!

Tesla reached out and tapped the sentence about the robot angel.

Nick blinked down at it, then gave his sister a look that said, "So?"

"That's our ticket in," Tesla whispered.

"Into where?" Nick asked.

Uncle Newt was still concentrating on his

Spaghettios, yet Tesla didn't dare say the words out loud. So she just mouthed them silently. She could tell Nick understood from the way his eyes went wide and his jaw slack.

"The scene of the crime," she'd said.

NICK AND TESLA'S

REPLACEMENT ROBO-ANGEL HOVERBOT

THE STUFF

- 2 foam or lightweight plastic disposable dinner plates (but not paper plates)
- 1 3-volt motor (available at electronics stores; the RadioShack catalog number is 273-223)
- 2 brass fasteners
- 1 paper clip
- Thin bell wire (also available at electronics stores)
- 1 plastic lid from a coffee can, a can of nuts, or a deli container
- 1 CR2 3-volt battery (available at most large pharmacies or at stores that sell cameras)
- 1 popsicle stick or unsharpened pencil
- Hot-glue gun
- Scissors
- Sharpened pencil
- Ruler
- Pushpin or thumbtack

THE SETUP

1. Draw a 3-inch-diameter (7.5-cm) circle onto the middle of one of the foam plates. (Using a soup can as a stencil might make this step easier.)

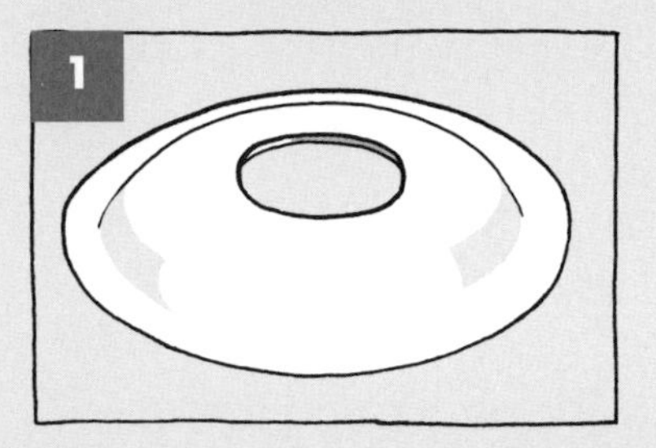

2. Use scissors to carefully cut out the circle.

3. Slip the paper clip over the point of one of the fasteners and then poke the fastener through the bottom of the plate.

4. Push the other fastener through the plate so that the paper clip can slide and touch the other fastener. This is your switch!

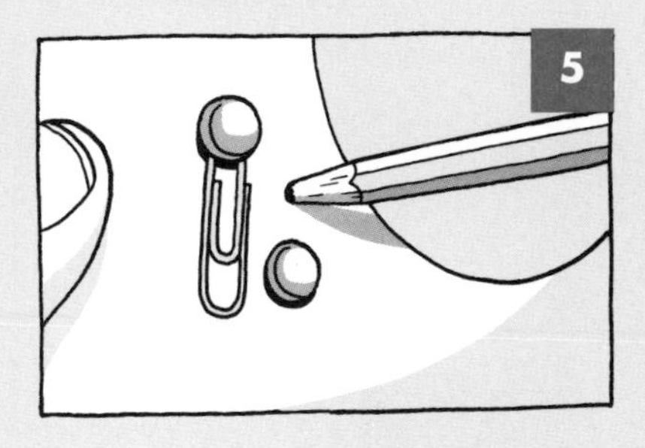

5. Use a pencil to poke a small hole through the plate for some wire to go through.

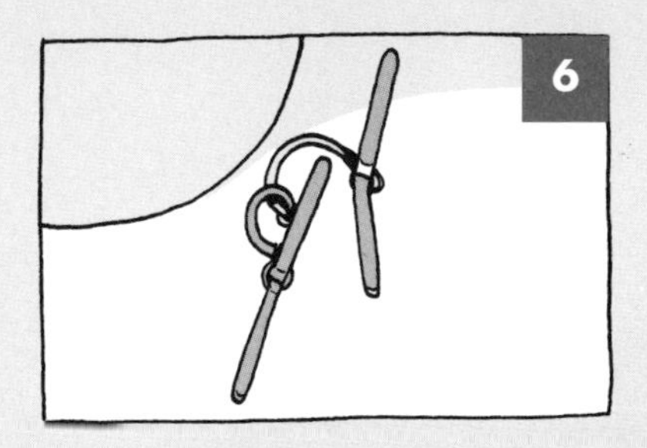

6. Strip about 1 inch (2.5 cm) from the ends of two wires. Then poke the wires through the hole from the top and twist

the ends around the fasteners as shown. (Make sure the two fasteners don't touch.)

7. If your motor already has wires attached to it, skip ahead to step 8. If not, cut two 8-inch (20.3-cm) lengths of bell wire and strip the plastic from the ends. Attach one end of each wire to the metal leads on the motor. Hot-glue them in place.

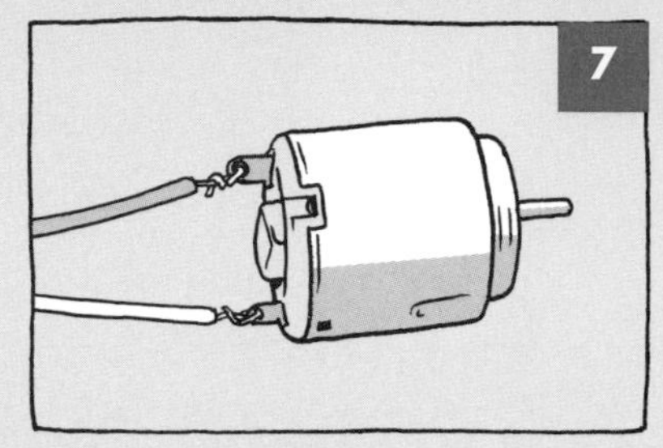

8. Cut out the propeller template on page 223. Trace the outline of the template onto the plastic lid, then cut out the propeller with scissors.

9. Use a pushpin or thumbtack to poke a small hole in the middle of the propeller.

10. Bend each blade on the propeller as shown on the template. The plastic should hold its shape after you bend it. If not, you will need to use a different lid.

11. Push the propeller about halfway onto the shaft of the motor and hot-glue it in place. Be sure the propeller has room to spin without touching the motor.

12. Cut two pieces from the other plate (or use cardboard if you have plastic plates) 1¾ inches (4.5 cm) high and 1½ inches (4 cm) wide. Hot-glue them in place on either side of the opening, as shown on page 162. These are the supports.

13. Hot-glue the popsicle stick or unsharpened pencil across the top of the supports.

14. Hot-glue the motor to the bottom side of the popsicle stick. The propeller should be just above the opening in the plate. Be sure it doesn't hit the supports or the plate when you spin it with your finger.

THE FINAL STEPS

1. Carefully tape one of the motor's wires to one end of the battery. Then tape one of the switch's wires to the other end of the battery. (Be sure the metal wire is exposed.)

2. Use a little hot glue to secure the battery to the top of the support.

3. Attach the two remaining wires to each other.

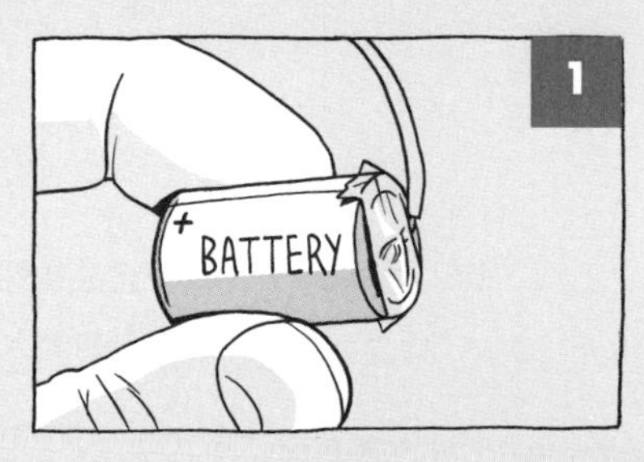

4. Now it's time to test the motor. To turn it on, rotate the paper clip so that it

touches both fasteners. The motor should spin and elevate the hoverbot. When the propeller spins, it should blow air downward. If the propeller is spinning the wrong way, just reverse the two wires attached to the battery.

5. If the motor doesn't spin, the wires are probably not connected somewhere. Check the wires on the motor and all other connections, and make sure you didn't hot-glue the motor shaft.

6. The small battery is lightweight, which is perfect for hovercrafts, but keep in mind that it won't last super long. So be sure to turn off the hovercraft when you're not using it.

7. Happy hovering!

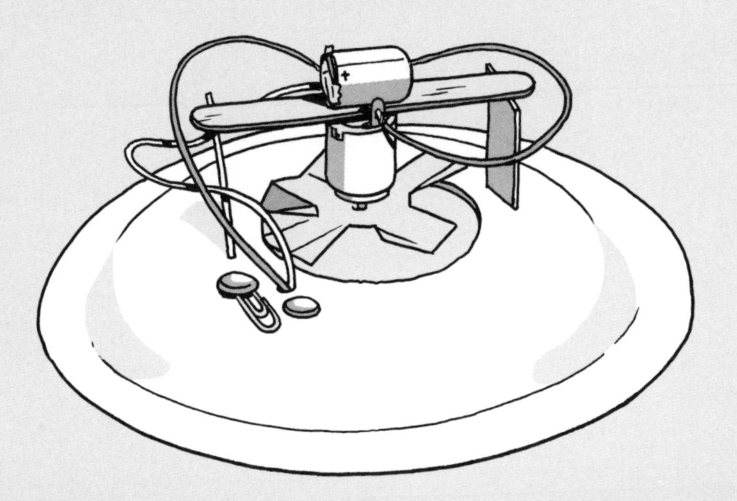

CHAPTER 11

"Remind me again why we need to build a robo-angel hoverbot," Nick said.

He and Tesla had been hunched over one of the worktables in the basement for an hour.

Tesla didn't even look up from the little motor she was carefully gluing in place.

"You know," she said.

And he did. For the most part.

The burglar who'd broken into Jewelry by Angela might be the same one who'd stolen Mr. Kuskie's comic book. In each case, the thief had gotten inside through mysteri ous, undetectable means and had made off with valuable items that had just arrived in the store. So Nick and Tesla needed an excuse to go to Jewelry by Angela and snoop around, and a replacement for the stolen robot angel they'd read about in the newspaper seemed like just the thing.

"But why a robo-angel *hoverbot*?" Nick asked. "The article didn't say anything about the robot angel flying."

Tesla squirmed but didn't answer.

"Come on," Nick prodded her. "Why a hoverbot?"

"I want ours to be cooler," Tesla mumbled.

Nick nodded, satisfied. "Thought so."

A few minutes later, Uncle Newt came down to the lab.

"You're not spending the afternoon with Dr. Sakurai again?" Tesla asked him innocently.

"She's busy with Wonder Hut stuff today. But we'll be getting together tonight," Uncle Newt said. "I'm thinking of giving her a peek at the Banana Vac 9000. Maybe letting her take it for a spin around the house. You know—as long as it doesn't get all explodey. What do you think? Romantic, huh?"

As he spoke, Uncle Newt went to the cooler in

which he kept the vacuum's fuel—thirty pounds of rotten bananas—and flipped up the lid.

A noxious cloud of banana gas and gnats spread through the basement.

"Maybe you should stick with dinner and a movie," Nick said after he was done coughing. "Most ladies probably wouldn't appreciate being asked to clean a guy's house."

"I'm not asking her to clean my house!" Uncle Newt protested. "I'm giving her the opportunity to alpha test an extremely exciting, innovative piece of technology!"

"By cleaning your house," Tesla said.

"No! Okay, yes. Well, kind of. But that's not the point. Listen—"

Uncle Newt opened his mouth to continue but then had to pause to pick a gnat off his tongue.

"Listen," he said again, "do you know what your mother and father's first date was?"

Nick and Tesla shook their heads.

"They went out for pizza," Uncle Newt said, "so they could discuss the paper they were working on together, about the use of positronium annihilation to power gamma ray lasers. They were so excited by their ideas that they forgot to eat . . . but the paper went on to win an Einstein Prize for Laser Science."

Nick slumped. He'd been looking forward to hearing about his parents—learning something new about the people he missed so much—and then his uncle had to go and mangle the story.

"Mom and Dad are agronomists," Nick said. "They never won the Einstein Prize for Laser Science."

Uncle Newt flapped a hand dismissively.

"Oh, well, not under their own names," he said, as if that explained everything.

Tesla opened her mouth to speak and then her face reddened and contorted grotesquely, and she sucked in a ragged breath and put her hands to her throat.

"Tez! Tez, are you okay?" Nick said, hurrying to her side.

Tesla looked at him with wide, watery eyes.

"I swallowed a bug," she croaked.

She started coughing. The hacking grew worse and worse as she sucked in more putrid banana gas between each cough.

Fortunately, the robo-angel had been ready for testing when Uncle Newt joined them in the lab.

Nick snatched it up and guided his sister toward the staircase.

"I don't know anything about romance," he said to Uncle Newt. "But I still don't think this is a great place for a date."

Tesla began coughing even louder, and Nick slapped her on the back as they scrambled up the steps and escaped to the kitchen.

Uncle Newt considered his nephew's dating advice for a moment, then shook his head and chuckled.

"Kids," he said, and he bent down and started scooping slimy black sludge into the Banana Vac's fuel sac.

After a minute on the back porch, inhaling deep lungfuls of fresh air, Tesla was finally able to speak.

"So," she said.

That's when Silas and DeMarco showed up.

"It's even worse than we thought," Silas said. "I heard my mom and dad talking last night, and it's not just the store we might lose. It's our house, too! *Please* tell me you've got good news."

"I'm sorry, Silas. We don't have any good news." Tesla looked down at the hoverbot, which Nick had put down on the patio. "But we're working on it."

"Well, we do have *some* good news," Nick said. "We were able to get that picture back into the Treasure Trove last night. But then things got weird."

He told Silas and DeMarco about the burglar in the jewelry store while Tesla got the hoverbot ready for its trial run.

"Aww, come on, guys!" Silas said when he heard that his friends might have spotted the comic book thief. "Why didn't you run over there and tackle the dude?"

"Uhh . . . 'cause we're kids and he is a dangerous criminal," Nick said.

"*I* would've tackled him," DeMarco said.

"Me, too!" Silas said.

"Then it's a good thing you weren't there, because you could've gotten yourselves killed!"

"Guys," Tesla said. "Chill."

"But—" Silas began.

He ended with a "whoa!"

The hoverbot was floating.

Tesla gave it a gentle push, and it went gliding

across the porch on a half-inch-high cushion of air.

"What is that?" DeMarco asked.

"An angel sent to bring us good news," said Tesla. "Or answers, anyway."

They made the hoverbot more angelic by painting wings and a haloed face on the Styrofoam and gluing a few cloudlike cotton balls around the edges. That was all the customizing they could do, though. Anything that added more weight would overwhelm the little motor and keep the hoverbot from floating.

As soon as the paint and glue were dry, Tesla carefully lowered the robo-angel into her backpack, and all four kids climbed on their bikes and set off for downtown Half Moon Bay.

They found Angela behind the counter at Jewelry by Angela. They knew it was her because the first thing she said when they walked in was, "Well, hi there! I'm Angela!"

She didn't look much like the stereotypical angel. She was short and plump, with frizzy red hair, and she wore an old-fashioned dress and cat's-eye glasses instead of white robes and a halo. But there was a cherubic quality to the way her big, friendly grin pushed her round cheeks almost over her eyes.

"What can I do for you?" she said.

A few yards beyond her on the right was a small office, the door open.

A few yards beyond her on the left was the store's shattered back door, which was being replaced by a workman in a blue jumpsuit.

The air in the store still smelled like smoke.

"We read about what happened last night," Tesla said. She set her backpack on the display case and started unzipping it. "We felt so bad we decided to make you this. To replace the one that was stolen."

Tesla pulled out their robo-angel and hooked up the battery.

The hoverbot began floating across the glass countertop.

"Oh, my!" Angela exclaimed. "Isn't that just darling! You made this yourselves?"

Nick and Tesla nodded. Silas did, too, though all he'd done was put a dab of glue on one of the cotton balls.

"Why, you're every bit as clever and sweet as that

Hiroko from the Wonder Hut," Angela said. She jerked her head to the side. "She brought me a new robot, too."

The kids turned to find a foot-high metal angel standing atop one of the store's other display cases. It was squat and blocky, with silver wings and a halo that pulsed from pink to purple to blue and back again. In one of its hands was a little harp.

"Walk up to it and you'll get a surprise," Angela said. "Go on. You'll love it!"

"All right," Tesla said.

She took a few steps toward the robot.

Its eyes began to glow red, and it turned its head as if to look at her.

"Are you a new customer?" the robot croaked in a low, electronic voice.

Tesla looked over her shoulder at Angela.

"Say yes," Angela said.

"Yes," said Tesla.

"The Hallelujah Chorus" began blasting from a speaker in its belly.

"Cute, huh?" Angela said when the music stopped.

"Yeah. Adorable," Tesla said. She turned to give

her brother a significant look.

"It can see," Nick said. "And hear."

Tesla nodded.

They both began looking around the store.

Their gazes stopped at the same spot, across the room from the robot. A small keypad was mounted on the wall there. One word was printed on it.

DependAlarm.

Nick and Tesla looked at each other, their wide eyes saying "aha!"

No one else noticed.

“I just wish these things were real,” Angela said, sending the hoverbot bouncing into the cash register with a gentle flick of the finger. “I could use a few guardian angels around here. I’m telling you—Half Moon Bay is going to the dogs. And I’m not just talking about me being robbed.”

“Oh, yeah?” said DeMarco.

Angela gave him a vigorous nod. “Yeah. Take the man who runs the antiques place across the street. Barry Dobek. I think he’s losing his mind. Yesterday, he started shouting about giant bugs in his store, but when the police showed up he was just stomping on wind-up toys!”

“Oh, yeah?” DeMarco said again.

“Yeah! Dobek claimed to have been robbed, too. But then whatever it was he thought was gone turned up in his store this morning covered in pigeon doody.”

“Oh, yeah?” DeMarco said.

It had become obvious that “Oh, yeah?” was all that was required to keep Angela talking.

“Yeah!” she said. “According to Dobek, someone tossed a bunch of bread or crumbs or something through an open window last night. The pigeons found them and started eating them and then flew around pooping on everything! He's going to be scrubbing the place for weeks!"

Angela burst into a cackle.

Nick and Tesla exchanged guilty glances. They knew then what happens when you throw a bunch of bagels into an antiques store.

Angela noticed their expressions and choked off her laughter.

"I know I shouldn't find it funny. But he's really not a very nice man. Gouges customers, is rude to the locals, never gives anything back to the community." Angela paused to consider Dobek's list of faults, then decided to add one more. "And he's an incorrigible gossip."

"Uhhh . . . excuse me?" said Nick, hesitantly raising a hand. "I hate to interrupt, but would you mind if I asked you a couple questions about last night?"

Angela smiled. "Curious about the cops and robbers, huh? That's only natural for a boy your age. As long as I don't have any customers, fire away."

"Thank you. I was wondering . . ." Nick nodded at the metal robo-angel standing on the countertop near Tesla. "Is that where you kept your old robot?

The one that was stolen?"

"Yes."

Nick turned to point at the keypad on the wall. "And are those the controls for your security system?"

"Yes." Angela rolled her eyes. "For all the good *that* did me."

"How does it work?" Nick asked.

"You mean how does DependAlarm *claim* it works?" Angela said. "Well, when it's activated, it's supposed to set off an alarm ten seconds after anyone enters or leaves the store. The delay is so I can go to the keypad and enter the code to turn it off. But that burglar last night opened my safe somehow, and that must have taken a lot more than ten seconds. Who knows how long he was rummaging around in here before the alarm finally sounded?"

We do, Nick and Tesla could have said. *And yes—it was a lot more than ten seconds.*

"Where is your safe?" Tesla said instead.

Angela furrowed her brow, suddenly looking doubtful about these strange kids and their nosy questions.

"I don't think I should say."

"Obviously, it's not in plain sight, though," Nick

said. "Have you ever talked about it to anyone in the store? Maybe even told someone the combination?"

"Well, I have employees who close up for me sometimes, so I've told them how to—wait. I get it now!"

"You do?" Nick said.

"Sure, I do. You kids want to be junior detectives. You're trying to solve the mystery." Angela's smile returned, wider than ever. "That is just the cutest thing ever!"

Tesla's face turned scarlet red. The expression on it was *not* the cutest thing ever. It wasn't cute at all.

"We're not *trying* to solve the mystery," she grated out through gritted teeth. "We *have* solved the mystery."

"Oh, you have?" Angela chuckled.

"Yeah," said Silas. "You have?"

Tesla nodded grimly.

"Hold on, Tez," Nick said. "It's just a hypothesis. We don't have any proof."

"I think we do, Nick." Tesla turned to the little robot angel Hiroko Sakurai had given Angela. "I think we have some right here."

She started to reach out for the robot.

"Back off, kid," it said in its distorted electronic voice.

Everyone froze.

"Did that thing just say 'Back off, kid'?" Angela asked.

"Yes," said DeMarco, eyes wide with disbelief. "Yes, it did."

"Back off or what?" Tesla said to the robot.

"You don't want to find out," it told her.

Tesla smiled. "Oh, that's where you're wrong."

She reached out for the robot again.

Four small, black, curved objects popped out of slots in its chest.

"What the heck are those?" Angela asked, her already high-pitched voice jumping up an octave.

She got her answer a moment later.

The robot took two tottering steps forward, then toppled off the countertop.

The second it hit the floor, it began zig-zagging quickly through the kids' feet.

"Wheels!" Nick cried as it whizzed by. "It's got wheels!"

Tesla took off after it. "Quick! We've got to catch it!"

The robot zipped to the back of the store—where

it was stopped by the new glass door.

"Aha! Got ya!" Tesla said. "You can't get away!"

The robot apparently agreed.

So instead it exploded.

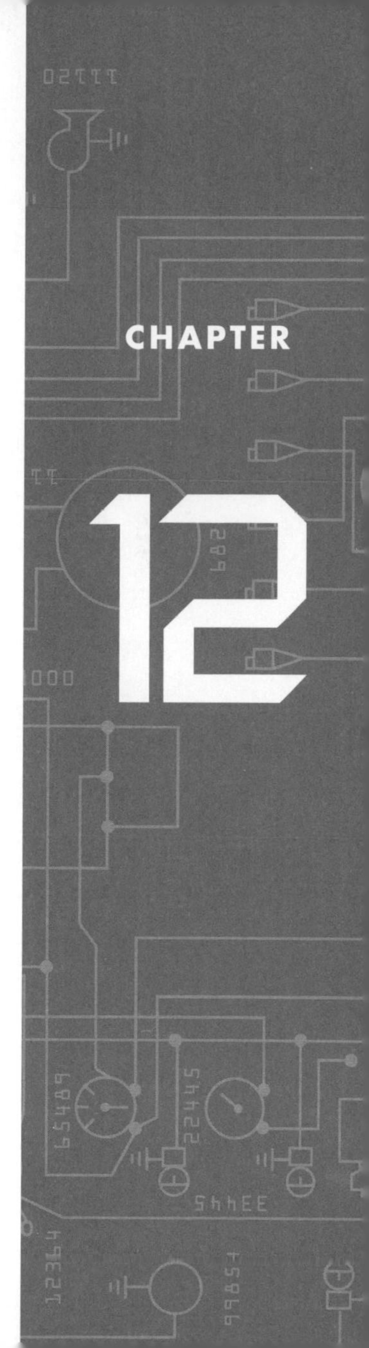

CHAPTER 12

It wasn't a huge explosion. Just big enough to destroy the robot angel and blow out the glass behind it.

When the smoke cleared, the kids could see the repairman on the other side of the ruined door. He must have been loading his truck, because he'd come running up with his keys still in his hand.

"Oh, man . . . I just fixed that!" he said. "What happened?"

"That's what I'm wondering," said DeMarco.

"Me, too," said Silas.

"And me," said Angela. "What the heck is going on?"

They all turned to Nick and Tesla.

"We know who broke into your store," Nick told Angela. He sounded sad rather than triumphant, though. "And Hero Worship, too."

"And we've got to do something about it. *Now*," Tesla added. "Before the thief destroys the rest of the evidence."

"What evidence do you—?" Silas began.

"The comic book!" DeMarco blurted out.

Tesla nodded.

"Oh, no!" Silas wailed. "Oh, no, no, *no*!"

"Uhhh . . . comic book?" Angela said.

"There's no time to explain," Tesla told her. "Sgt. Feiffer should be here soon."

"Ish," Nick threw in.

The sergeant could be anywhere in town, and his little three-wheeled squad car couldn't go much faster than a golf cart.

"Whenever he gets here," Tesla said to Angela, "have him come meet us at the Wonder Hut."

Angela frowned. "The Wonder Hut? Surely you don't think . . . ?"

She looked from the shattered door to the alarm control pad to the display case where the angel had been standing.

"Oh. Oh, I see," she said. "That first angel wasn't stolen at all, was it?"

Tesla shook her head. "No. It blew up, just like this one. That's how she got in. Then she turned off the alarm, took her time stealing what she wanted, and turned the alarm back on so that no one would know she'd learned the code."

"Wait," said Silas. "*She?*"

"The thief," Nick said. "Dr. Hiroko Sakurai."

"You mean the Wonder Hut lady?" Silas's eyes went wide. "No way."

"Way," said Tesla. "And it's time to stop her."

She spun and bolted for the store's front door, with Nick, DeMarco, and Silas right behind her.

"What's the plan?" Nick asked Tesla as they rushed up Main Street.

"Who says we need a plan?" DeMarco said. "We'll just run in and grab her."

"Right." Silas nodded firmly and cracked his knuckles. "Then we'll tickle her till she tells us where the comic book is."

"Guys, that *is* a plan," Nick pointed out. "A really bad one."

"Why?" DeMarco asked.

"Because Dr. Sakurai's got exploding robots and she probably knows we're coming."

"Oh. Right."

"I still think the tickling would work," Silas said.

"Could you guys just be quiet and let me think for half a block?" Tesla snapped.

The boys went silent.

It took them nine seconds to go half a block.

"So?" Nick said.

"Okay," said Tesla, "here's what we're going to do . . ."

Tesla and DeMarco marched into the Wonder Hut with all the confidence they could muster. Between the two of them, they could muster a lot. That's why they were the two marching in.

Still, Tesla couldn't help but feel a little queasy as she locked eyes on Dr. Sakurai.

She was reading something spread out on the countertop near the cash register. Lining the shelf behind her were what Tesla now knew to be her minions. Her own private robot army.

Dr. Sakurai had been busy. There were even more propeller-topped robots than the day before. A dozen in all, packed in around the robot pirate she'd tried to give Barry Dobek for the Treasure Trove.

Would she send them swarming at Tesla and DeMarco the second she saw them? Or would she try to play it cool? Keep wearing a friendly mask until it was torn away by the truth?

Dr. Sakurai looked up and locked eyes on Tesla.

"Why, just who I wanted to see!" she said with a smile. "Do you guys know anything about Pokémon?"

So, cool it is, Tesla thought. *Well, we'll just have to heat things up a little.*

"Uhhh, Pokémon?" DeMarco said, sounding thrown. He'd come into the Wonder Hut ready for a confrontation, not a conversation about kids' games.

"Yeah. I'm thinking of stocking trading cards, but I have no idea what's popular anymore," Dr. Sakurai said pleasantly. "There are so many listed in this catalog I don't even know where to start."

"I'll tell you where to start," Tesla said. "With why you did it."

Dr. Sakurai cocked her head to the side, a look of puzzlement on her face.

"Why I decided to start selling Pokémon cards?" she said.

"Oh, please," Tesla sneered. "Skip the innocent act. We know why you've been giving robots to all the businesses in town."

"Because they're good publicity?" Dr. Sakurai said.

"Because they're good spies!" DeMarco barked. "That's how you knew Mr. Kuskie had *Stupefying* #6. That's how you knew where to find his spare keys. And that's how you got into Jewelry by Angela!"

"*What?*" Dr. Sakurai's expression shifted from bewilderment to concern. "Are you two all right? You're sounding a little . . . confused."

Tesla crossed her arms and tried to look stern.

"This is pathetic, Dr. Sakurai," she said. "It's too late for bluffs, and you should know it. You saw us in the jewelry store through your little spy. You even spoke to us through it, before you blew it up. So why keep pretending?"

"I'm not pretending anything. I honestly don't

know what you're talking about." Dr. Sakurai started to walk around the counter. "Why don't you two come back to the stockroom and have a seat and a cool drink while I—"

"No!" Tesla said, moving to block Dr. Sakurai behind the counter. "Just tell the truth! Why use your genius for evil? Why steal? *Why break our uncle's heart?*"

"Ooooo," said Silas. "Sounds like it's getting dramatic out there."

He crept to the black curtains that hung in the doorway to the Wonder Hut's stockroom, parted them an inch, and peeped out at the store.

"*Silas*," Nick hissed. "*Get away from there.*"

"All right, all right."

Silas turned and went back to searching the dark, cramped, cluttered room. He and Nick had snuck in through the back door a minute earlier, while Tesla and DeMarco distracted Dr. Sakurai. But so far all they'd found were stacks of models and chemistry sets and kites and the like, along with a desk covered with bills, some cleaning supplies and tools in a corner, and a pile of dusty PVC pipes outside the teeny staff bathroom.

Curiosity the robot stood nearby. Even though it was turned off and motionless, its control pad abandoned on the desk, it still gave Nick the creepy feeling that they were being watched.

"I thought Dr. Sakurai was going to admit everything right off the bat," Silas said, lifting a mop and peering down into the bucket it had been sitting in. "You know, 'Yes! It was me all along! I did it because blah blah blah!' Like the villains always do in comic books so the good guy has time to figure out how to defeat them."

"In the real world, people aren't that dumb," Nick whispered as he rifled through the folders in a filing cabinet. All he saw were order forms and more bills. "But that's fine. The longer Dr. Sakurai drags this out, the more time we'll have to look for the comic book, right?"

"I guess." Silas put down the mop and began inspecting a grungy pink duster feather by feather. Picking good places to search obviously wasn't his strong suit. "You know what worries me, though?"

"What?"

"What if Dr. Sakurai's denying everything because she knows there's no proof? What if she already got rid of the rings and stuff from the robbery last night? What if the comic book has already been destroyed?"

Then your dad's store is doomed and you're probably losing your home, too, Nick thought.

"Let me give *you* a 'What if?'" he said. "What if the comic book is right here in this room, only we're so busy talking that we end up losing our chance to find it?"

"Hmmm," Silas said. "Good question."

He put down the feather duster and started rooting through a garbage can.

At least that was an improvement. Sort of. In a useless kind of way.

Then again, who was Nick to judge? He hadn't found anything either.

He opened the last drawer in the filing cabinet, then sighed.

It was empty.

Dr. Sakurai still hadn't cracked, and Tesla was growing tired of badgering her.

"Please believe me," Dr. Sakurai said. "None of this makes any sense to me."

Tesla shook her head sadly. "Why do you keep lying? The proof is all over town."

"What do you mean?"

"The robot superhero in Hero Worship, Incorporated," said DeMarco. "It's still there—with the camera and microphone inside that you used to spy on Mr. Kuskie."

"Exactly. And the robot chef in Ranalli's Italian Kitchen is probably wired up the same way," Tesla said. "All we have to do is go get them, and we'll have proof that you didn't build them for free publicity. You built them to eavesdrop on people."

"But, Tesla—I didn't build those robots at all."

"Oh, sure," Tesla said. "Then where did they come from? They didn't just hatch out of little metal eggs."

"You're right about that," someone chuckled. "I built them."

Tesla, DeMarco, and Dr. Sakurai all turned toward the voice.

Duncan, the Wonder Hut's roly-poly assistant

manager, was standing just inside the front door. In his arms were four small, silver shapes.

A robot chef, a robot superhero, a robot police officer, and a robot dog.

He put them on the floor in a little line, all facing Dr. Sakurai and the kids. Then he locked the front door and flipped the sign that hung from it. Instead of telling people outside "COME IN, WE'RE OPEN," it now told them "SORRY! WE'RE CLOSED."

"Wonderful, aren't they?" Duncan said, looking down at his robots. "I went around town collecting them once I knew you kids had made the connection between them and the robberies. Told everyone that Dr. Sakurai wanted to make some improvements. As if she could!"

Duncan was wearing a parka that was far too big and bulky for such a warm summer day, and he reached into one of its oversized pockets and pulled out a black box about the size of a textbook. There were buttons and levers on one side, and Duncan took hold of a little metal nub on one edge and pulled out a foot-long antenna. Then he started pushing buttons.

The robots on the shelf behind Dr. Sakurai began

to hum, their little eyes glowing.

"Giving the robots away was *my* idea, wasn't it, Dr. Sakurai?" Duncan said. "And you were more than happy to steal credit for my work—just like you were happy to steal away the store that should have been mine!"

"I wasn't trying to steal credit for anything, Duncan," Dr. Sakurai said, her soft voice trembling. "I was following your advice. Trying to build relationships around town, just like you said. As for the store, I didn't know it was yours to steal."

"*WELL, YOU SHOULD HAVE!*" Duncan roared. "*IT WAS ME WHO KEPT THIS PLACE ALIVE ALL THESE YEARS! ME! AND NOW IT'S ME WHO'S GOING TO KILL IT!*"

Tesla and DeMarco both leaned a little away from the man, as if his ravings were a hurricane blowing them backward.

"Whoa," DeMarco said to Tesla under his breath. "This guy's really flipping out."

"Whoa," Silas said to Nick under his breath. "This guy's really flipping out."

They both were peeking through the curtains at the scene unfolding in the store.

The little bald assistant dude, Duncan, was ranting about how he'd worked at the Wonder Hut forever and had earned the right to buy it when the original owner retired. Yet just because he didn't have as much money as *Dr. Sakurai* (he spat out the name with a face-twisting scowl), he'd lost his chance. But it wasn't over yet, because he wasn't going to let some snooty NASA big shot make him feel like a nobody.

"I'm so sorry, Duncan," Dr. Sakurai said. "I had no idea I was being snooty."

"You weren't," said Tesla.

"*SHUT UP!*"

Duncan jabbed at the buttons on the control pad in his hand, and the robotic chef, superhero, cop, and dog started marching toward Tesla and DeMarco.

Duncan pushed another button, and the propellers on the robots on the shelf began to spin.

Dr. Sakurai squeaked with fright and ran out from behind the counter as, one by one, the robots began to rice into the air.

"These robots are the only proof that any spying's been going on," Duncan said. "I built them just like my little angels. With microphones. Cameras. Everything."

"See! I told you!" Silas gloated to Nick. "He's going to explain his whole scheme!"

The robots took up positions around Dr. Sakurai, Tesla, and DeMarco, some standing on the floor, others hovering just off the ground.

"*Everything*," Duncan said again.

Nick turned away from the curtain. Silas didn't seem to realize what *everything* meant, but he did.

The other robots were built with self-destruct devices, too. Each one was a little mobile bomb. And soon—any second, even—Duncan meant to set off those bombs. Individually, the explosions would be dangerous but not necessarily deadly. All together, though . . .

Nick put a hand to his chest, clutching at the star-shaped pendant that hung there beneath his shirt. If, as he and Tesla suspected, it really was a tracking device—a link to his mom and dad's mysterious friend, Agent McIntyre—then there must be some way to activate it or use it to send an S.O.S.

There was no time to figure it out, though. Agent

McIntyre wouldn't be coming to the rescue. It was up to Nick to save his sister and DeMarco and Dr. Sakurai.

Nick frantically scanned the stockroom for something, *anything* he could use to head off disaster. But how was he supposed to stop an army of exploding robots? What could a couple kids like him and Silas do to—?

Hey.

Nick's gaze settled on the PVC pipes piled up outside the bathroom.

Maybe. Just maybe . . .

He hurried across the room and got to work.

NICK'S

TOTALLY IMPROVISED SUPER-SOAKER BOT BLASTER

THE STUFF

- 1 24-inch (61-cm) piece of PVC pipe (labeled "1¼")
- 1 6-inch (15.2-cm) piece of PVC pipe (labeled "1 inch")
- 1 end cap for the PVC pipe
- 1 T connector for the PVC pipe
- 1 1¼-inch-diameter (3.2-cm) wood dowel, 25 inches (63.4 cm) long
- 2 1-inch pan head screws
- 1 ¼-inch-wide Fender washer
- Rubber gasket material
- Drill
- Screwdriver
- Hammer
- Sandpaper
- Electrical tape

Tip: Ask if the hardware store sells scrap pieces of PVC pipe. You might find the right sizes, and they'll be cheaper than having pieces cut to order.

THE SETUP

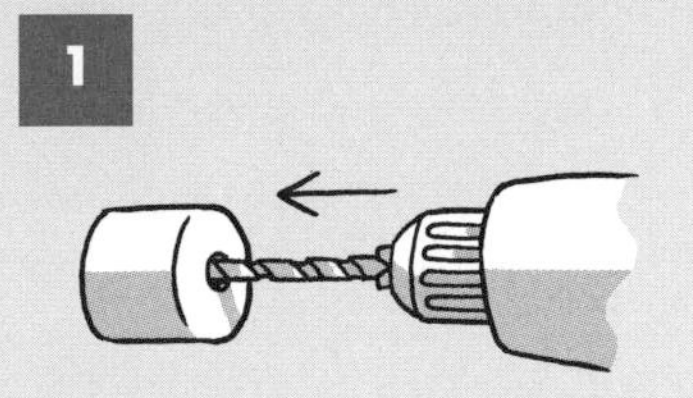

1. Drill a ³⁄₁₆-inch (0.5-cm) hole into the center of the end cap.
2. Use the Fender washer to trace three circles onto the rubber gasket material.

3. Cut out the circles very carefully, taking your time. Each rubber disk should be slightly larger than the Fender washer.
4. Using the Fender washer as a guide, carefully poke a hole in the center of each rubber disk with the screw.

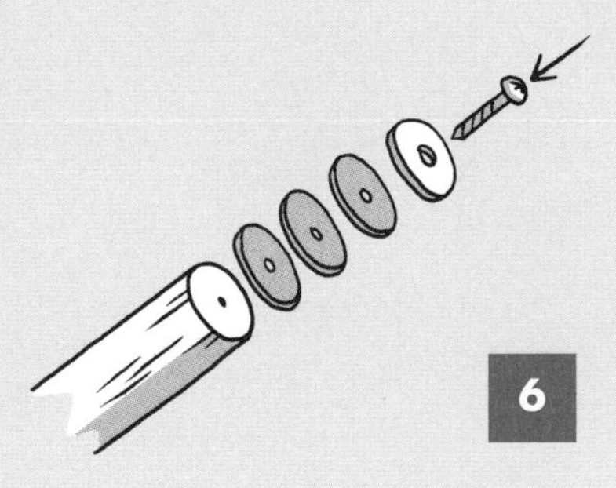

5. Again using the Fender washer as a guide, mark the exact center of the end of the wooden dowel.
6. Stack the rubber gaskets, and then use the washer and screw to attach them to the end of the dowel, as shown. This is the plunger.

7. Test-fit the plunger in the PVC chamber; it should not be too easy or too hard to push and pull the plunger through the chamber. If the plunger is too big or drags along the inside of the chamber, use the sandpaper to sand down the rubber disks a little bit at a time until you have a snug and even fit.

8. Wrap a few layers of electrical tape around the rubber disks while pulling the tape taut. Test-fit the plunger as you go along. You can adjust the fit by adding or removing electrical tape as needed.

9. Place the T connector over the other end of the dowel and drill a pilot hole for a screw.

10. Secure the T connector to the dowel with a screw.

11. Attach the smaller (1-inch) piece of PVC pipe to the T connector to make a handle. Secure it by using either a hammer to tap it into place or PVC cement (with the help of an adult).

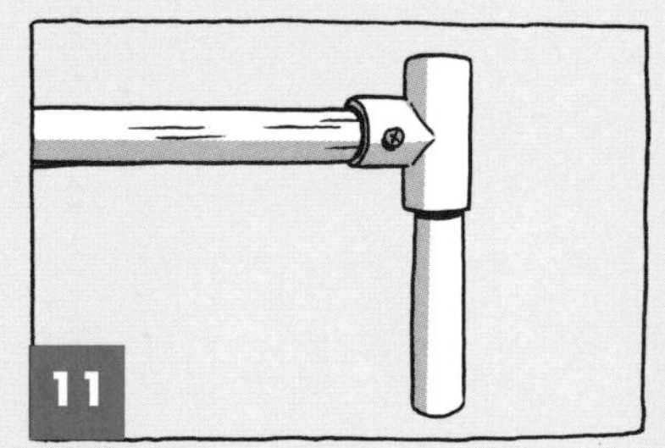

12. Use the hammer to tap the end piece onto one end of the chamber to fit securely. If it doesn't stay on or if it leaks, have an adult use PVC cement to attach it permanently.

THE FINAL STEPS

1. Place the end of the blaster under water and pull back slowly on the plunger handle. Air pressure will cause the chamber to fill with water. (Don't pull the plunger too far or it will come out!)

2. To fire, aim the blaster and push the plunger into the chamber. The harder you push, the farther the water jet will go!

3. If your blaster leaks or doesn't pull up water, add electrical tape to the plunger for a better seal or make new rubber disks that are a little wider.

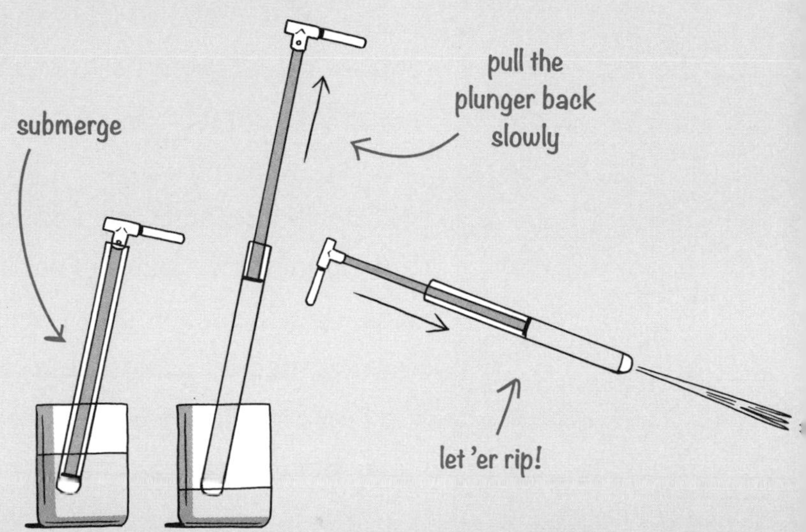

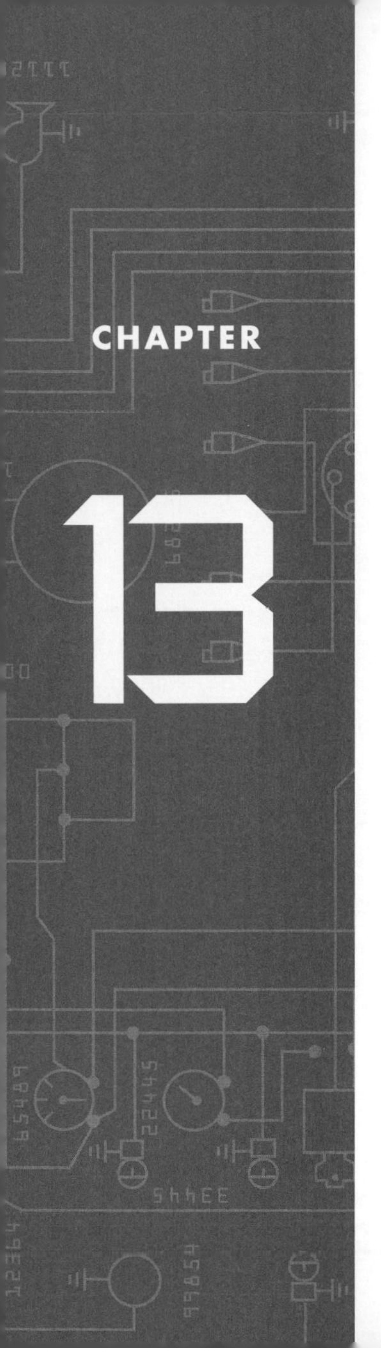

CHAPTER 13

"So after I'd sold off that comic book and the jewelry and whatever else I could steal," Duncan said, "I was going to burn down the Wonder Hut and use the money to start my own hobby shop." The pudgy little man's gaze went distant, dreamy. "The Marvel Shed. Sounds a lot cooler than 'The Wonder Hut,' don't you think?"

Tesla, DeMarco, and Dr. Sakurai all nodded nervously. They were clustered in the middle of the store surrounded by robots, some looking up at them from the floor, others hovering nearby like little helicopters.

Tesla had hoped to stall for time by complimenting Duncan on his robotics and asking admiring questions about his fiendishly clever scheme. Only she hadn't needed to say a word.

Duncan had spent the past five minutes talking through his entire plan, complete with a long, detailed description of his struggles to find a Wi-Fi booster powerful enough to reach his apartment from Main Street but small enough to fit in a robotic dog. (The robot dog had been a pain, but what else could he build for a place called Poochie Pizzazz Pet Grooming?)

Now that he was done with his story, he rubbed his chin pensively.

"Well," he said, "that about covers it. I guess this is the point where I'm supposed to say, 'And I would've gotten away with it, too, if it weren't for you yada yada yada, etc., etc.' Only I *am* getting away with it. Ha!"

Duncan started walking backward, toward the front door. He brought up the control pad in his hands and prepared to push a big red button.

"Wait!" Tesla cried. "You didn't tell us how you . . . uhhh . . . how you . . . uhhh . . ."

"Knew the combination to the jewelry store safe!" DeMarco said.

"Oh, yes!" Dr. Sakurai chimed in. "I've been wondering about that!"

"Well, it should be obvious," Duncan told them. "I was listening in when the lady who owns the place told her . . . hey." Duncan shook a finger—the one that had been about to hit the self-destruct button—at his prisoners. "You're just stalling, aren't you?"

Tesla, DeMarco, and Dr. Sakurai all gave him innocent "Who us?" looks.

"Oh, no, no, *no*!" they said.

"We really, truly haven't figured everything out yet," Tesla added.

"All right, then. I might as well tell you, since you're all about to—" Duncan cut himself off with an abrupt shake of the head. "*Nah*. I really should get going."

He looked down at the control pad in his hands.

"No!" said Tesla.

"Don't!" said Dr. Sakurai.

"Flerbel jerz!" said DeMarco, who wasn't even sure what he was trying to say but felt like he should say *something*. He'd never had to come up with last words before, and now that he actually needed some he'd messed them up.

"Flerbel jerz?" said a puzzled Duncan.

Then he shrugged and moved his finger toward the big red button.

Tap tap tap.

Duncan froze.

He was so close to victory. So close to revenge. So close to escape.

And now someone was knocking on the door a half step behind him.

Whoever it was, they rapped again on the glass. Hard.

"Stay right there," Duncan told Tesla, Dr. Sakurai, and DeMarco.

He turned to peek around the SORRY! WE'RE CLOSED sign.

Standing outside, a metallic hand raised to knock on the door again, was Curiosity the robot.

"Well," Duncan said, "I didn't expect *that*."

Curiosity crashed its hand through the glass and grabbed Duncan's control pad. Duncan managed to keep a hold on it, though, and he and the robot began playing tug-of-war through the doorframe.

"Run!" someone yelled.

Duncan looked over his shoulder and saw the girl's brother, Dick or Rick or Mick, charge out of the back room with the big kid whose dad owned the comic book shop.

Dick/Rick/Mick was holding Curiosity's controls.

The big kid was holding a length of white pipe as if it were a rocket launcher.

The two other kids and Dr. Sakurai were making a break for it, darting past the robots all around them.

"Nooooooo!" Duncan howled. "You're not getting away!"

He wrenched the control pad away from Curiosity and stabbed a finger at the self-destruct button.

Click, went the control pad.

Nick opened his eyes.

Without meaning to, he'd squeezed them shut when he'd seen Duncan push the button on the control pad.

Only the robot army didn't blow up. Didn't send flames and smoke and metal and plastic spewing through the store. Didn't do anything, actually, but start talking.

"Arrrrrr! Thank ye for setting sail for the Treasure Trove, me hearties!" said the robot pirate.

"Woof woof! It's a dog's life at Poochie Pizzazz!" said the robot dog.

"Crime does not pay, evildoer!" said the robot superhero.

"Dang," said Duncan. "Hit the wrong button."

Dr. Sakurai and Tesla and DeMarco had escaped up the store aisles, but they weren't out of danger yet.

Duncan fiddled with the controls, and his robots took off after Dr. Sakurai and the kids, some zipping along the ground, others whooshing through the air.

"Now, Silas!" Nick shouted.

He jammed forward the throttle toggles on Curiosity's control pad, and the robot smashed through the rest of the glass door and crashed into Duncan's back.

Silas, meanwhile, was pumping hard on the super soaker, sending jets of water spraying over one robot after another.

The robot superhero began to sizzle.

The robot cop threw off sparks.

The robot chef simply stopped in its tracks.

The robot pirate fell over with an "Arrrrrrrrrr."

The hover-bots crackled and sputtered and nose-dived into display racks and model kits and the floor.

One final robot—the little metal dog—managed to corner Tesla and Dr. Sakurai against a collection of model railroad switches and bridges. Silas turned the super soaker on it, but all that came out was a thin trickle and a fine, fizzy mist.

The super soaker was out of water.

"Finally!" Duncan crowed, fighting off Curiosity with one hand while holding up his control pad with the other. "It's showtime!"

He managed to push the red button with his thumb.

The robo-dog shook and hissed and smoldered.

A wisp of white smoke emerged from its butt, and then it went still.

Even just a trickle and a mist from the super soaker had been enough to fry the robot's circuits.

"Awwww, man," Duncan moaned. "What the—?"

"The water's got sodium chloride in it," Nick

explained. "From a chemistry set I found in the back room."

"You don't want to know where we got the water," Silas said. Then he added in a stage whisper: "*The toilet.*"

"So you made a saline solution to short out the robots," said Tesla. "Nice one, Nick!"

Nick grinned. "Thanks."

"Hey! I did all the shooting!" Silas said.

Duncan threw his control pad at him.

"Keep congratulating yourselves, suckers!" he spat as Silas ducked aside. "I'm still getting away with your precious comic book!"

He whirled around and started for what was left of the front door—just as Sgt. Feiffer stepped through it.

"Uhhh . . . hi, kids," the sergeant said, surveying the broken glass and salty puddles and ruined robots strewn all around him. "Angela said you needed to see me about something?"

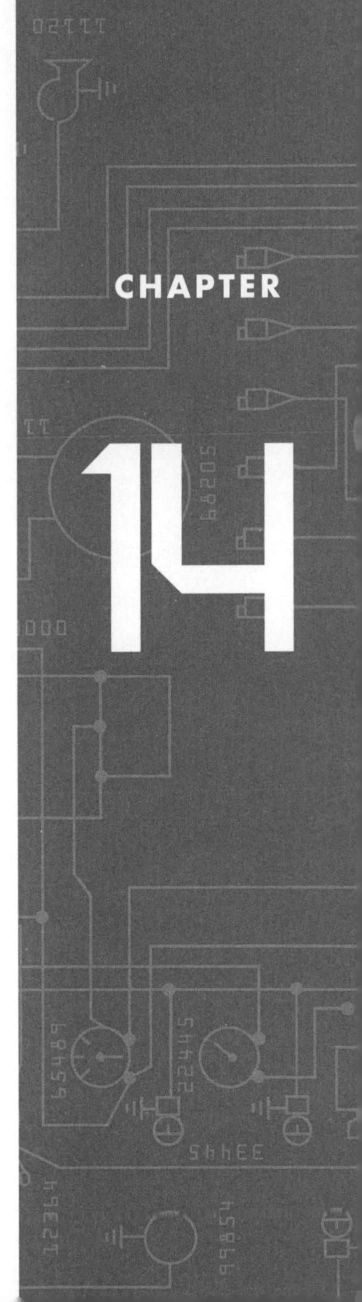

CHAPTER 14

It took a little time to sort things out. Everyone had to walk down the block to Half Moon Bay police headquarters (because Sgt. Feiffer's little scooter-cart could carry only one person at a time) and answer a *lot* of questions.

Fortunately, Duncan was still in a talkative mood, and he admitted everything from his seat on the lone bunk in the police station's teeny holding cell.

"Apparently, the surveillance video he shot with his robots is on the computer in his apartment," Sgt. Feiffer told the kids. "He says everything he stole is there, too."

"Including *Stupefying* #6?" Silas asked.

Sgt. Feiffer nodded. "I'll be picking everything up as soon as I can get a search warrant. Your dad'll have his comic book back by the end of the day tomorrow."

"Hero Worship, Incorporated is saved!"

Silas *woo-hoo*ed and turned to high-five DeMarco.

DeMarco managed to put his hand up and smile feebly, but he couldn't *woo-hoo*, too.

"What's the matter?" Silas asked him. "We solved the mystery and caught the bad guy."

"And ended up at the police station waiting for our parents to come get us. For the second time in two weeks," DeMarco said. "My mom's not going to let me out of the house till the first day of school." He looked over at Nick and Tesla, who were sitting beside him in the waiting room. "It's been nice knowing you."

They all shook hands grimly, as if they'd never see one another again. And indeed when DeMarco's mother and father came to get him, the glares they gave Nick and Tesla said it all.

DeMarco might have broken more than one bone riding his bike down slides and trying to parachute off roofs with umbrellas. But until he'd met Nick and

Tesla, he'd never been mixed up with real-life *criminals* before. These new kids were trouble.

DeMarco's parents hustled him away as if Nick and Tesla were radioactive.

Silas's dad, on the other hand, burst in with a grin on his face and his big arms opened wide.

"Forget Metalman!" he exclaimed as he crushed Nick and Tesla and Silas in a bear hug. "From now on, you guys are my biggest heroes. Thank you!"

"You're welcome," Nick and Tesla wheezed.

It was unclear if Mr. Kuskie heard them, though, because their faces were smooshed deep into his broad chest at the time.

Before leaving with his son, Mr. Kuskie told Nick and Tesla their money was no good in his store. They could come in for free comics whenever they wanted.

"Too bad we don't like comic books," Tesla said after he was gone.

Nick shrugged. "Maybe they'll grow on us. Free is free."

At last, they were alone in the waiting room with Hiroko Sakurai—she'd insisted on staying until all the kids had been picked up—and for the tenth time Tesla turned to her and apologized.

And for the tenth time, Dr. Sakurai said it wasn't necessary.

"The robots I gave away were spying on people," she said. "Of course you were going to think I was up to no good. I'm just glad you caught Duncan before he could destroy the Wonder Hut or sell off Mr. Kuskie's comic book." Dr. Sakurai's expression turned wry and sly. "And I think it's sweet that you were mad at me for supposedly breaking your uncle's heart."

Tesla squirmed in her seat. Apologies made her uncomfortable enough without dragging *that* into it.

"He really does like you," Nick told Dr. Sakurai. "A lot."

Dr. Sakurai nodded.

"I'd guessed," she said.

"Hey, ho!" Uncle Newt bellowed as he burst into the police station. "Who's up for It's-Froze-Yo!?"

For some reason, trouble always seemed to make him hungry.

Dr. Sakurai stood and started toward him.

"Sorry, Newt—I need to get back to the Wonder Hut," she said. "I still have to figure out how I'm going to lock up for the night with no front door. Plus I have a dozen or so wet, dead robots to clean up."

"Oh, no, you don't!" Newt said. "*We* have a dozen or so wet, dead robots to clean up. I need to get Nick and Tesla home, but I'll come straight to the store as soon as I can."

"And Tez and I can come by tomorrow if there's still more to do," Nick added.

"Yeah—we really ought to help clean the place up," said Tesla.

Dr. Sakurai smiled. "Thanks. I'd like that."

Like Mr. Kuskie, Dr. Sakurai gave Nick and Tesla hugs—though separately, and not hard enough to crush any ribs—and then said good-night and left.

"'A dozen or so wet, dead robots'?" Uncle Newt mused. "I don't know what the heck you two have been up to, but it sounds like fun!"

"I guess you could call it that," said Tesla.

"If you consider being terrorized by exploding robots fun," muttered Nick.

"As a matter of fact, I do," said Uncle Newt. "But that's another story." He wrapped his arms around the kids' shoulders and started guiding them toward the door. "You can tell me *yours* on the way home."

Trouble might have made his uncle hungry, but it made Nick very, *very* tired. He nearly fell asleep while Tesla explained what had happened.

When they got to the house, Uncle Newt said simply, "Well, that was quite a day, wasn't it?" Then he grabbed the last stale bagel off the counter and headed out the door again, bound for the Wonder Hut.

As Nick stumbled toward the stairs to the bedroom he and Tesla shared, he was mulling over plans for an automatic pigeon-poop scooper. (He felt guilty about the mess they'd made in the Treasure Trove.) His brain was too fuzzy to work out the details, though, and he was practically snoring as he took the first step up the staircase.

Yet still, worn out as he was, he stopped and turned around when he remembered the nightly rite he'd almost skipped.

He shuffled off to the kitchen, picked up the phone, and punched up voicemail.

Suddenly Nick was wide awake.

"Tez! You've got to hear this!"

"What is it?"

Nick answered her by pushing some buttons on the phone and then holding it up between them.

"Message left today, 5:16 p.m.," a robotic voice droned.

Nick had turned on the speakerphone.

"Tesla! Nick!" a woman said. "There's so much I want to tell you, but there's no time!"

Tesla dropped her Pop-Tarts.

The woman was their mother.

"Everything's more . . . complicated than we led you to believe," she said. "We sent you to your uncle to keep you safe. But you're not. The people we were trying to hide you from know where you are. They might even be there already. Whatever you do, don't trust—"

There was a burst of crackling static, then a beep.

The call had been cut off.

"It's not fair!" Nick wailed. "Why'd she have to call when we were gone?"

Tesla had no answers. In fact, all she had were more questions.

Why did their parents think they were in danger? Who were she and Nick not supposed to trust? Who were the "they" who meant them harm?

And when would they be coming for Nick and Tesla?

HERE'S A SNEAK PREVIEW OF

NICK AND TESLA'S SECRET AGENT GADGET BATTLE

by "Science Bob" Pflugfelder and Steve Hockensmith

SNOOPING AROUND BOOKSTORES IN MAY 2014!

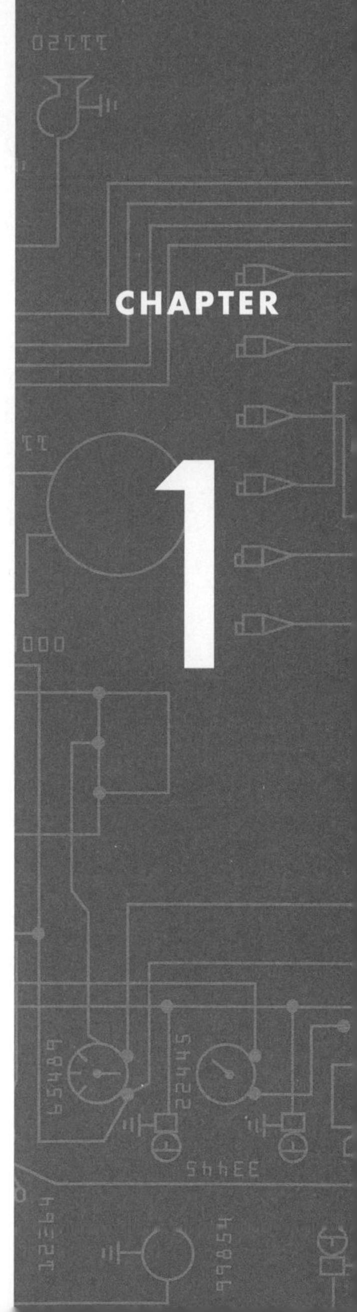

"It's her," Nick said. "She's the spy."

"Who is?" said Tesla.

She looked around. She and her brother were in their uncle's backyard about to test-fly the hoop glider they'd been working on that morning. There was only one other person in sight: a fortyish woman crouched over a bed of begonias about forty feet away. She was wearing jeans and a T-shirt and dirty gardening gloves.

She didn't look much like a spy to Tesla.

"You mean Julie Casserly?" Tesla said.

Nick nodded.

"She's always watching us," he said. "Always glaring."

"Wouldn't you if you lived next door to Uncle Newt?"

As if on cue, Julie turned to glower at them.

"What's that?" she said, jabbing a trowel at the glider in Tesla's hands. "A remote-controlled spear?"

Tesla looked down at the glider. It was just a couple hoops of stiff paper, a small one in front and a larger one behind, connected by a straw.

"No," said Tesla.

"A computerized javelin?" said Julie.

"No."

"A self-shooting arrow?"

"No."

"Some kind of missile?"

"No. It's a glider."

Julie narrowed her eyes. "And what's that supposed to do?"

"Uhh . . . glide," said Tesla.

Julie cocked her head, her lips twisting into a tight, sarcastic smile.

"Yeah, right," she said. She pushed herself off her

knees and began walking away. "Let me get inside before you set it loose. I don't want to be here when it 'glides' someone into the hospital."

The woman stomped around the corner of her house and disappeared.

"Not very brave for a spy," Tesla said.

"Maybe that's just her cover," Nick muttered. "Anyway, go ahead. Try the glider."

Tesla brought the glider up, pointed it away from Julie's yard, and launched it with a flick of the wrist. It shot away with surprising speed and flew smoothly over Uncle Newt's lawn, arcing to the left as it went.

"Whoa! Look at it go!" said Nick.

"And go and go and go," said Tesla.

She'd expected the glider to fly five yards, tops. Yet even after twenty it was still six feet off the ground and not slowing down. In fact, it was soaring toward some trees on the other side of Uncle Newt's property, perhaps about to fly out of the yard altogether.

"Hey, kids!" a cheerful voice called out. "Whatcha up to?"

It was Uncle Newt's other neighbor, Mr. Jones,

stepping out onto his patio. The paunchy gray-haired man always had a smile and a wave for Nick and Tesla.

Unfortunately, it was a really bad time for a smile and a wave.

"Mr. Jones!" Nick cried out. "Duck!"

"A duck? Where?"

Mr. Jones gazed up into the sky.

The glider came swooping through the trees and smacked him in the face.

Nick and Tesla ran up to the old man as he staggered back into his house.

"Where did that crazy duck go?" he started to say.

Then he saw the hoop glider lying in the doorway.

"Oh," he said.

"We're sorry, Mr. Jones," Nick said.

"We had no idea it would fly that far," said Tesla.

Mr. Jones rubbed his bulbous (and now red) nose.

"No harm done," he said.

He didn't sound like he meant it, though, and the smile he gave the kids when he handed back their glider seemed strained.

Mr. Jones closed the door on Nick and Tesla, grumbling something about getting an ice pack.

“Great,” Tesla said as she and her brother trudged away. “The one neighbor who’s nice and we go and throw a paper airplane up his nose.”

“It was an accident,” Nick said. “And who’s to say Mr. Jones is such a nice guy anyway?”

“What?”

Tesla looked over at her brother, thinking he might be joking.

Nick hadn’t been joking much lately, though. And he *never* joked about this.

“It’s him,” Nick said. “He’s the spy.”

“Mr. Jones? He must be, like, two hundred years old.”

“Spies get old just like normal people.” Nick threw a suspicious squint over his shoulder. “He’s always watching us. Always smiling.”

“So now being nice makes someone a suspect?”

“Maybe. You remember what Mom said in her message. There’s someone here we can’t trust. We have to be careful.”

“There’s ‘careful’ and then there’s ‘paranoid.’”

A squirrel scampered across the lawn in front of them.

Tesla pointed at it.

"Watch out! A spy!"

"Come on, Tez. I'm not being *that* bad."

A car honked in the distance.

Tesla cupped a hand to her ear.

"Hark! A spy!"

"Okay, okay. I get it. I'm going overboard."

Tesla pointed at herself. "Oh, my gosh! Right next to you! Spy!"

"Geez, Tez—I said I get it."

Tesla smiled.

"Good. I know that message was scary, but there's nothing to freak out about. I'm sure things aren't nearly as bad as they sounded. I mean, what kind of spy is going to waste his time on a couple kids?"

Nick nodded glumly, looking unconvinced.

Tesla wasn't convinced herself, but she wasn't going to show it.

"Now let's get a new straw for the glider and try it again," she said. "And no more obsessing about spies, all right?"

"All right," Nick sighed.

He and Tesla crossed the patio and entered the back door.

A huge man in a trench coat and fedora was

waiting for them in Uncle Newt's kitchen. He was holding something long and shiny and sharp in his right hand.

"So. We meet at last," the man said in a deep, heavily accented voice. "I have questions for you two. And for your sakes, I hope you have the right answers. . . ."

About the Authors

"SCIENCE BOB" PFLUGFELDER is an award-winning elementary school science teacher. His fun and informative approach to science has led to television appearances on the History Channel and *Access Hollywood*. He is also a regular guest on *Jimmy Kimmel Live*, *The Dr. Oz Show*, and *Live with Kelly & Michael*. Articles on Bob's experiments have appeared in *People*, *Nickelodeon* magazine, *Popular Science*, *Disney's Family Fun*, and *Wired*. He lives in Watertown, Massachusetts.

STEVE HOCKENSMITH is the author of the Edgar-nominated Holmes on the Range mystery series. His other books include the New York Times best seller *Pride and Prejudice and Zombies: Dawn of the Dreadfuls* and the short-story collection *Naughty: Nine Tales of Christmas Crime*. He lives with his wife and two children about forty minutes from Half Moon Bay, California.

NICK AND TESLA'S

REPLACEMENT ROBO-ANGEL HOVERBOT PROPELLER TEMPLATE

(see pages 158–162)

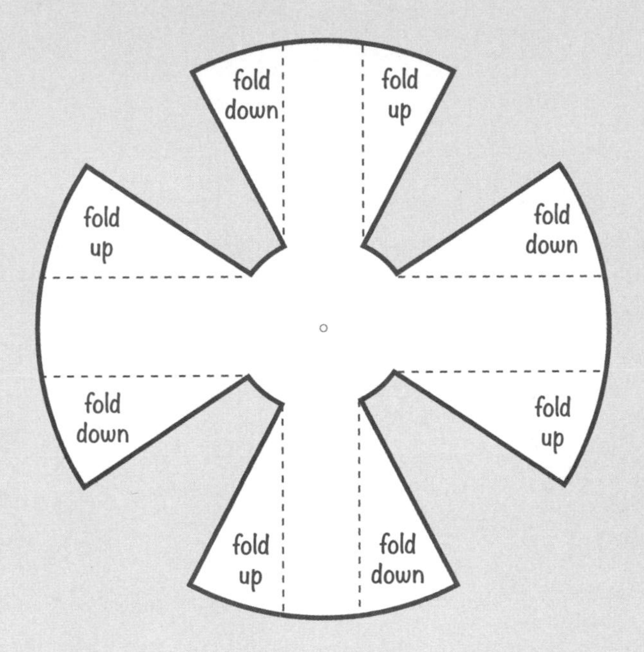

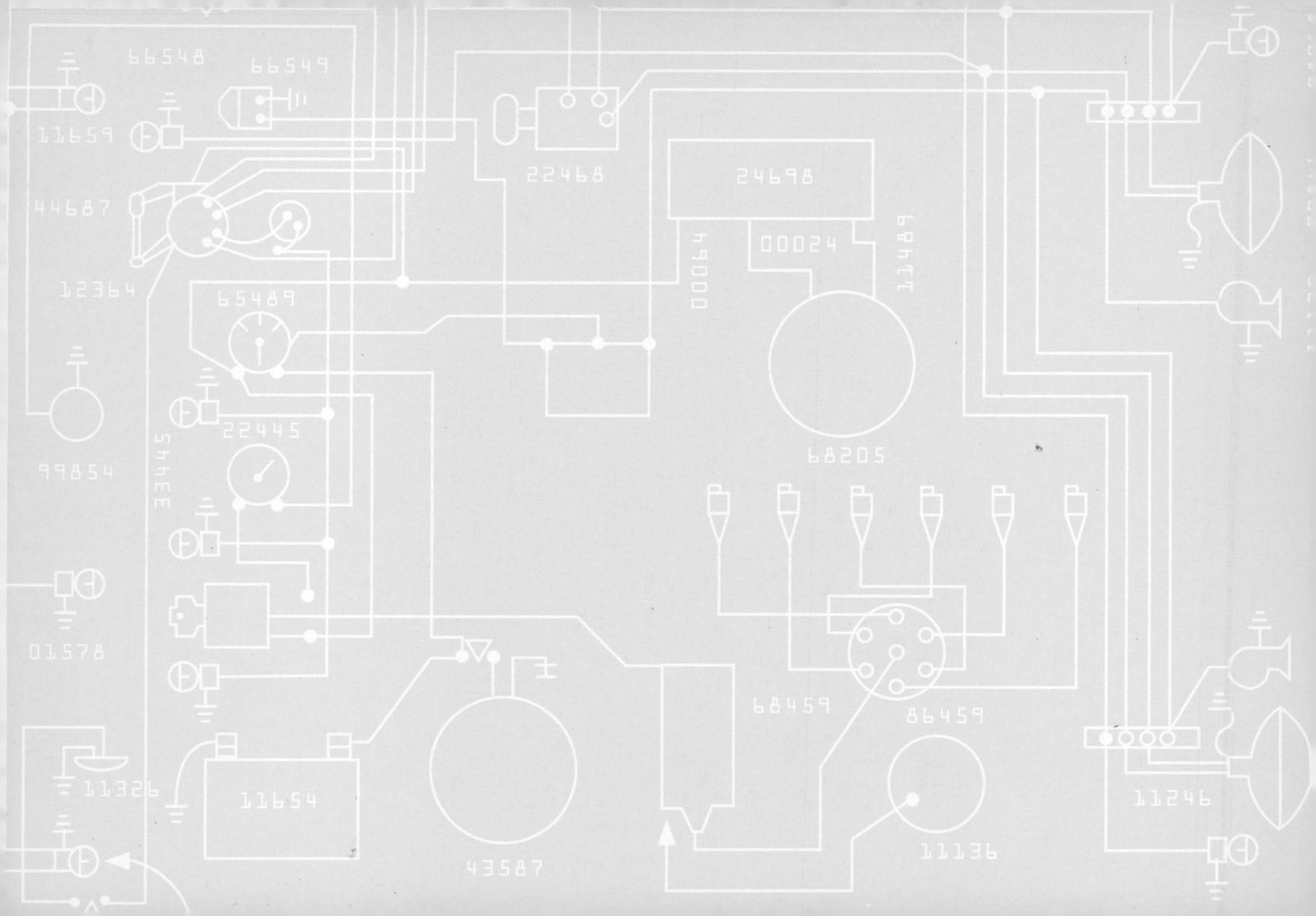
66548
66549
11659
22468
24698
44687
00024
12364
65489
22445
68205
99854
01578
68459
86459
11326
11654
43587
11136
11246